Ten Science Fiction Stories

Edited by

R. A. BANKS MA PhD

HODDER AND STOUGHTON
LONDON SYDNEY AUCKLAND TORONTO

For Hervé

ISBN 0 340 21371 X

Printed in Great Britain for
Hodder and Stoughton Educational,
a division of Hodder and Stoughton Ltd,
Mill Road, Dunton Green, Sevenoaks, Kent,
by Clarke, Doble & Brendon Ltd, Plymouth.

TEN SCIENCE FICTION STORIES

Contents

Acknowledgments

For permission to use copyright material in this book, the editor and publishers wish to thank the following: A. P. Watt & Son and the Estate of H. G. Wells for 'In the Abyss' from *The Short Stories of H. G. Wells*; The Society of Authors as the literary representative of the Estate of E. M. Forster for 'The Machine Stops'; Dennis Dobson Publishers for 'Robot AL-76 Goes Astray' from *The Rest of the Robots* by Isaac Asimov; David Higham Associates Ltd for 'Compassion Circuit' by John Wyndham (from *Spectrum IV*, published by Michael Joseph and Pan Books), an extract from *Expedition to Earth* by Arthur C. Clarke, and 'The Sentinel' from *The Best of Arthur C. Clarke, 1937–1971* (both published by Gollancz and Sphere Books); Faber and Faber Ltd for an extract from *The Inheritors* by William Golding; and Mr Howard Fast for his story *The Large Ant*.

Introduction

If we really want to live, we'd better start at once to try:
If we don't, it doesn't matter, but we'd better start to die.

W. H. Auden

One of the major themes of modern Science Fiction is the search of mankind for the ideal – the ideal man or woman, government, state, world, or universe. The theme can be traced back a long way in literary history: the Greek philosopher, Plato, writing in the fourth century BC, explored in his Dialogues what he would expect to find in the best of all possible worlds; *The Republic* examines the philosophical ideas underlying the concept of an ideal state; the account of the fabulous island of Atlantis in *The Timaeus* and *The Critias* describes the land as one of great beauty where the people live in prosperity until the sea swallows it up because of the wickedness of its inhabitants.

In 1516 Sir Thomas More published at Louvain the Latin edition of his *Utopia*, 'Nowhere Land'. The basis of it might have been suggested by the voyages of Amerigo Vespucci, who claimed to have discovered in 1497 'Terra Firma', a strange land set far to the west of Europe and one now thought to be the continent of South America. In Antwerp More met a traveller, Raphael Hythloday, who said that he had discovered a marvellous country where there was a real community of feeling, war was avoided, different religions were tolerated, and the laws were just. To give such a description was implicitly to comment on the condition of life in More's own Tudor England:

> 'so he rehersyde manye actes and constytutyons wherby thies our cytyes, natyons, contreys, and Kyngdomes may take ensample, to amende theyre faultes, enormytyes and errours.'

In its earliest days Utopian literature had discovered that to describe an ideal state was in itself a way of making a statement about the imperfect systems of government and the corruption of daily life in one's own time.

The development of this form of literature has continued almost without a break in England until the twentieth century. Bishop Hall's *Mundus alter et Idem* (1607), Bacon's *New Atlantis* (1626), James Harrington's *The Commonwealth of Oceana* (1656) developed the line, but it was Defoe's *Robinson Crusoe* (1719) which made the first interesting satirical deviation from the tradition. In 1704 Alexander Selkirk, the son of a shoemaker, ran away to sea and joined an expedition led by Captain William Dampier. Selkirk asked to be put ashore on the uninhabited island of Juan Fernandez, where he remained until he was rescued five years later. Defoe used the account of Selkirk's adventures as the basis for *Robinson Crusoe*, whose hero is given the opportunity to establish a new order for himself in a new land. Perversely he merely sets about re-creating the very society from which he has managed to escape. The chance of Utopia has been rejected.

Swift's satire of his own times is bitingly clear in *Gulliver's Travels* (1726). The inhabitants of Lilliput are merely six inches high and everything on the island is similarly scaled down. The feuds, the pompous behaviour, and the needless war they wage with their neighbours across the Channel therefore seem petty and ridiculous. In contrast, in Brobdingnag, where the people are as tall as steeples, the king tells Gulliver, who has proudly related the achievements of his own country without being aware of the impression he is making,

> 'I cannot but conclude the bulk of your natives to be the most pernicious race of little odious vermin that nature ever suffered to crawl upon the surface of the earth.'

The flying island of Laputa and its neighbouring continent of Lagado continue the satire, this time directed at men of science and the 'projectors' such as those who created the famous South Sea Bubble. The work concludes with an account of the land of the Houyhnhnms, a race of simple but virtuous horses contrasted with the brutal Yahoos who bear the shape of men.

Samuel Butler's *Erewhon* (an anagram of 'nowhere') published in 1872 and *Erewhon Revisited* (1901) are in the same satirical tradition of the traveller – this time to New Zealand – who sees his own world indirectly as he looks at another. W. H. Hudson's *A Crystal Age* (1906) narrated the adventures of a botanist on an expedition who is stunned by a fall amongst some rocks and comes to his senses in a pleasant land where the animals are surprised to find such a stupid human amongst them. Alice in *Alice's Adventures in Wonderland* (1865) and *Through the Looking Glass* (1872) had similarly moved from her own world into a land of make-believe, where strange incidents and strange creatures commented indirectly on the life and thoughts of Victorian times. Aldous Huxley's *Brave New World* (1932) and his essays in *Brave New World Revisited* (1959) have continued the Utopian tradition of discussing man's predicament in a hostile world by presenting an alternative society.

Themes other than that of Utopia go to make up the complex world of Science Fiction. As long ago as 1580 Sir Philip Sidney, soldier, courtier, author, and terrestrial traveller, provided a definition of a poet which might well describe the skills of many a modern writer of Science Fiction:

> 'He doth grow in effect another nature, in making things either better than Nature bringeth forth, or quite anew, forms such as never were in Nature, as the heroes, demi-gods, cyclops, chimeras, Furies, and such like; so he goeth hand in hand with Nature, not enclosed within the narrow warrant of her gifts, but freely ranging within the zodiac of his own wit.'
>
> *(An Apologie for Poetry)*

Science Fiction often begins with the credible and the possible to encourage the reader's later 'willing suspension of disbelief'. H. G. Wells's story *In the Abyss*, included in this anthology, seems to pay respect to scientific details at the start, but rapidly moves into the realms of the imagination. A writer of this kind of story cannot spend too long on explaining how the problems of prolonged inter-planetary travel, or of moving backwards or forwards through time, or of descending into the depths of the sea, or of using English to talk to bug-eyed monsters, can be solved; he needs to move on with his story and the reader must accept certain conventions. Most of us need only a little encouragement to adopt the framework of the writer who at least makes a gesture in the direction of science claiming to be concerned only with accurate and verifiable facts.

Advances in recent years have made some Science Fiction themes seem less remote. RTGs (Radioisotope Thermoelectric Generators), TOPS (Thermoelectric Outer Planet Spacecraft), STAR (Self-test and

Repair computer) and TARP (Test and Repair Processor) are a few of the developments which may make journeys to Jupiter possible later this century. Journeys to the Moon are no longer fantasy, but works like Cyrano de Bergerac's *Voyage dans la lune* (1550), Johan Kepler's *Somnium* (1634) and Bishop Godwin's *Man in the Moon or a Discourse of a Voyage thither by Domingo Gonzales* (1638) still have an appeal, if it is only to compare fiction with fact. So far science has not allowed man to travel to the centre of the Earth (cf. Jules Verne's *Voyage au centre de la terre*, 1864), although it has given him the power to travel round the world in fewer than the eighty days taken by Jules Verne's heroes in *Le tour du monde en 80 jours* (1873) or to circumnavigate the Earth under the sea more easily than the submariners of Verne's *Vingt mille lieues sous les mers* (1869). He still cannot travel through time (cf. *The Time Machine*, 1895), or make himself invisible (cf. H. G. Wells's *The Invisible Man*, 1897), or create human life from the dead (cf. Mary Shelley's *Frankenstein*, 1818 – a book which, incidentally, introduces the themes of the mad scientist and the researcher who lacks a proper sense of responsibility).

Jules Verne's writings and the early works of H. G. Wells dominated Science Fiction stories in the early twentieth century. The technological details of Verne and the stories of wonder and fear by Wells inspired tales of stranger lands and stranger creatures. Even Tarzan finds himself drawn into the world of science fantasy in Edgar Rice Burroughs's *Tarzan at the Earth's Core* and *Tarzan and the Ant Men*. Since 1945 the market for stories loosely – or firmly – based on science has been seemingly unsatiable, encouraged no doubt by satellites, interplanetary probes, the legend of the Unidentified Flying Object, the Russian and American achievements in Space, and Arthur C. Clarke's 2001, *A Space Odyssey*.

In this collection of stories I have tried to assemble some of the best examples of Science Fiction and Science Fantasy which explore many of the traditional themes of the genre: Utopian exploration, the search through the world or outside it for a better land, androids, robots, visits by aliens, machines against men, the destruction of the individual's own personality, the world of fear and the world of humour. Any selection must carry with it an arbitrariness which will offend some, make others question the implicit definition of the genre, but perhaps encourage many to enter and explore this strange realm of Science Fiction on their own journey of discovery. It is not necessarily an idle expedition:

'Some science fiction really does deal with issues far more serious than those realistic fiction deals with: real problems about human destiny.'

(C. S. Lewis in *Spectrum* IV, p. 15, an anthology edited by Kingsley Amis and Robert Conquest, 1966)

R.A.B.

Glubbdubdrib and Luggnagg

JONATHAN SWIFT

Jonathan Swift (1667–1745) was born at Dublin after his father's death. He was educated at Kilkenny Grammar School and Trinity College, Dublin, where he found himself in trouble because of offences against discipline; he was awarded his degree only on special consideration. He became Secretary to Sir William Temple and it was at this time that he began to write some of his poetry. He returned to Ireland and was ordained in 1694, but rejoined Temple two years later at Moor Park. In 1699 Swift went again to Ireland and was given a prebend in St Patrick's and the living of Laracor; he became dean of St Patrick's in 1713. After writing some political pamphlets he came back to England in 1726, the year in which Gulliver's Travels *was published. He paid his last visit to England in 1727, and spent the rest of his life in Ireland. About 1738 the symptoms of an illness (vertigo) from which he suffered all his life became marked and for a time before his death in 1745 he seemed to lose his reason altogether.*

The extracts which follow include some of the major themes taken up by later writers of science fiction: the passage of the writer through time – here the characters are made to exist out of time, although they are allowed to speak only about their own periods – the difficulties of communicating with those discovered on strange voyages or those who have been long dead; the nature of the immortals. Technically the writer leads the reader to suspend his disbelief by moving him gradually to accept the picture of the past; already Swift (or Gulliver) has transported him from Europe into the strange world of Glubbdubdrib and Luggnagg by means of a recognizable form of journey, and only then does he take the next steps into fantasy. Space and time are both destroyed in order that, by implication, the reader can see his own contemporary period more clearly. This oblique approach allows him to understand the satirical points: values have been distorted, past villains have succeeded, past good men have been banished, past cowards have become the heroes and past traitors have distorted the truth, but it is the present which has made the rogues of the past into good men and the good men of the past into rogues. How, then, can the judgments of the present be trusted? Who are the 'good' men now? Who are the 'rogues' now? What are the standards by which we must judge?

The success of Swift's approach largely depends on the point of view of his narrator: Gulliver is the interested observer who directs the reader's view, but seems not to condition it. He cannot refrain from making direct comments, however, and it is at such points that the reader's willingness to accept Swift's comments becomes strained. Provided the fiction is maintained, the satire can work.

'Glubbdubdrib', as nearly as I can intepret the word, signifies the Island of Sorcerers or Magicians. It is about one third as large as the Isle of Wight, and extreamly fruitful: it is governed by the head of a certain tribe, who are all magicians. This tribe marries only among each other; and the eldest in succession is prince or governor. He hath a noble palace, and a park of about three thousand acres, surrounded by a wall of hewn stone twenty foot high. In this park are several small inclosures for cattle, corn and gardening.

The governor and his family are served and attended by domesticks of a kind somewhat unusual. By his skill in necromancy, he hath power of calling whom he pleaseth from the dead, and commanding their service for twenty-four hours, but no longer; nor can he call the same persons up again in less than three months, except upon very extraordinary occasions.

When we arrived at the island, which was about eleven in the morning, one of the gentlemen who acccompanied me, went to the governor, and desired attmittance for a stranger, who came on purpose to have the honour of attending on his Highness. This was immediately granted, and we all three entered the gate of the palace between two rows of guards, armed and dressed after a very antick manner, and something in their countenances that made my flesh creep with a horror I cannot express. We passed through several apartments between servants of the same sort, ranked on each side as before, until we came to the chamber of presence, where after three profound obeysances, and a few general questions, we were permitted to sit on three stools near the lowest step of his Highness's throne. He understood the language of Balnibarbi, although it were different from that of his island. He desired me to give him some account of my travels; and to let me see that I should be treated without ceremony, he dismissed all his attendants with a turn of his finger, at which to my great astonishment they vanished in an instant, like visions in a dream, when we awake on a sudden. I could not recover my self in some time, until the governor assured me that I should receive no hurt; and observing my two companions to be under no concern, who had been often entertained in the same manner, I began to take courage; and related to his Highness a short history of my several adventures, yet not without some hesitation, and frequently looking behind me to the place where I had seen those domestick spectres. I had the honour to dine with the governor, where a new set of ghosts served up the meat, and waited at table. I now observed my self to be less terrified than I had been in the morning. I stayed until sun-set, but humbly desired his Highness to excuse me for not accepting his invitation of lodging in the palace. My two friends and I lay at a private house in the town adjoining, which is the capital of this little island; and the next morning we returned to pay our duty to the governor, as he was pleased to command us.

After this manner we continued in the island for ten days, most part of every day with the governor, and at night in our lodging. I soon grew so familiarized to the sight of spirits, that after the third or fourth time they gave me no emotion at all; or if I had any apprehensions left, my curiosity prevailed over them. For his Highness the governor ordered me to call up whatever persons I would chuse to name, and in whatever numbers among all the dead from the beginning of the world to the present time, and command them to answer any questions I should think fit to ask; with this condition, that my questions must be confined within the compass of the times they lived in. And one thing I might depend upon, that they would certainly tell me truth; for lying was a talent of no use in the lower world.

I made my humble acknowledgments to his Highness for so great a favour. We were in a chamber, from whence there was a fair prospect into the park. And because my first inclination was to be entertained with scenes of pomp and magnificence, I desired to see Alexander the Great,* at the head of his army just after the battle of Arbela; which upon a motion of the governor's finger immediately appeared in a large field under the window, where we stood. Alexander was called up into the room: it was with great difficulty

* See Notes on page 25.

that I understood his Greek, and had but little of my own. He assured me upon his honour, that he was not poisoned, but dyed of a fever by excessive drinking.

Next I saw Hannibal* passing the Alps, who told me he had not a drop of vinegar in his camp.

I saw Caesar and Pompey* at the head of their troops just ready to engage. I saw the former in his last great triumph. I desired that the Senate of Rome might appear before me in one large chamber, and a modern representative, in counterview, in another. The first seemed to be an assembly of heroes and demi-gods; the other, a knot of pedlars, pick-pockets, highwaymen, and bullies.

The governor, at my request, gave the sign for Caesar and Brutus to advance towards us. I was struck with a profound veneration at the sight of Brutus; and could easily discover the most consummate virtue, the greatest intrepidity, and firmness of mind, the truest love of his country, and general benevolence for mankind in every lineament of his countenance. I observed with much pleasure, that these two persons were in good intelligence with each other; and Caesar freely confessed to me, that the greatest actions of his own life were not equal by many degrees to the glory of taking it away. I had the honour to have much conversation with Brutus; and was told, that his ancestor Junius,* Socrates,* Epaminondas,* Cato the Younger,* Sir Thomas More,* and himself, were perpetually together: a sextumvirate to which all the ages of the world cannot add a seventh.

I was chiefly disgusted with modern history. For having strictly examined all the persons of greatest name in the courts of princes for an hundred years past, I found how the world had been misled by prostitute writers, to ascribe the greatest exploits in war to cowards, the wisest counsel to fools, sincerity to flatterers, Roman virtue to betrayers of their country, piety to atheists, chastity to sodomites, truth to informers. How many innocent and excellent persons had been condemned to death or banishment, by the practising of great ministers upon the corruption of judges, and the malice of factions! How many villains had been exalted to the highest places of trust, power, dignity, and profit!

The day of our departure being come, I took leave of his Highness the Governor of Glubbdubdrib, and returned with my two companions to Maldonada, where, after a fortnight's waiting, a ship was ready to sail for Luggnagg.

* See Notes on pages 25–6.

The Luggnaggians are a polite and generous people, and although they are not without some share of that pride which is peculiar to all eastern countries, yet they shew themselves courteous to strangers, especially such who are countenanced by the court. I had many acquaintance among persons of the best fashion; and being always attended by my interpreter, the conversation we had was not disagreeable.

One day in much good company, I was asked by a person of quality, whether I had seen any of their Struldbruggs, or Immortals. I said I had not; and desired he would explain to me what he meant by such an appellation, applyed to a mortal creature. He told me, that sometimes, although very rarely, a child happened to be born in a family with a red circular spot in the forehead, directly over the left eye-brow, which was an infallible mark that it should never dye. The spot, as he described it, was about the compass of a silver threepence, but in the course of time grew larger, and changed its colour; for at twelve years old it became green, so continued until five and twenty, then turned to a deep blue; at five and forty it grew coal-black, and as large as an English shilling; but never admitted any farther alteration. He said these births were so rare, that he did not believe there could be above eleven hundred Struldbruggs of both sexes in the whole kingdom, of which he computed about fifty in the metropolis, and among the rest a young girl born about three years ago. That, these productions were not peculiar to any family, but a meer effect of chance; and the children of the Struldbruggs themselves, were equally mortal with the rest of the people.

I freely own my self to have been struck with inexpressible delight upon hearing this account: and the person who gave it me happening to understand the Balnibarbian language, which I spoke very well, I could not forbear breaking out into expressions perhaps a little too extravagant. I cryed out as in a rapture; 'Happy nation, where every child hath at least a chance for being immortal! Happy people who enjoy so many living examples of antient virtue, and have masters ready to instruct them in the wisdom of all former ages! But, happiest beyond all comparison are those excellent Struldbruggs, who being born exempt from that universal calamity of human nature, have their minds free and disingaged, without the weight and depression of spirits caused by the continual apprehension of death.' I discovered my admiration that I had not observed any of these illustrious persons at court; the black spot on the forehead, being so remarkable a distinction, that I could not have easily overlooked it: and it was impossible that his Majesty, a most judicious prince, should not provide himself with a good number of such wise and able counsellors. Yet, perhaps, the virtue of those reverend sages was too strict for the corrupt and libertine manners of a court. And we often find by experience, that young men are too opinionative and volatile to be guided by the sober dictates of their seniors. However, since the king was pleased to allow me access to his royal person, I was resolved upon the very first occasion to deliver my opinion to him on this matter freely, and at large by the help of my interpreter; and whether he would please to take my advice or no, yet in one thing I was determined, that his Majesty having frequently offered me an establishment in this country, I would, with great thankfulness accept the favour, and pass my life here in the conversation of those superior beings the Struldbruggs, if they would please to admit me.

The gentleman to whom I addressed my discourse, because (as I have already observed) he spoke the language of Balnibarbi, said to me with a sort of a smile, which usually ariseth from pity to the ignorant, that he was glad of any occasion to keep me among them, and desired my permission to explain to the company what I had spoke. He did so; and they talked together for some time in their own language, whereof I understood not a syllable, neither could I observe by their countenances what impression my discourse had made on them. After a short silence, the same person told me, that his friends and mine (so he thought fit to express himself) were very much pleased with the judicious remarks I had made on the great happiness and advantages of immortal life; and they were desirous to know in a particular manner, what scheme of living I should have formed to my self, if it had fallen to my lot to have been born a Struldbrugg.

I answered, it was easy to be eloquent on so copious and delightful a subject, especially to me, who have been often apt to amuse my self with visions of what I should do if I were a king, a general, or a great lord: and upon this very case, I had frequently run over the whole system how I should employ my self, and pass the time if I were sure to live for ever.

That, if it had been my good fortune to come into the world a Struldbrugg; as soon as I could discover my own happiness, by understanding the difference between life and death, I would first resolve by all arts and methods whatsoever, to procure my self riches: in the pursuit of which, by thrift and management, I might reasonably expect in about two hundred years, to be the wealthiest man in the kingdom. In the second place, I would from my earliest youth, apply my self to the study of arts and sciences, by which I should arrive in time to excel all others in learning. Lastly, I would carefully record every action and event of consequence that happened in the publick, impartially draw the characters of the several successions of princes, and great ministers of State; with my own observations on every point. I would exactly set down the several changes in customs, languages, fashions, dress, dyet and diversions. By all which acquirements, I should be a living treasury of knowledge and wisdom, and certainly become the oracle of the nation.

I would never marry after threescore, but live in an hospitable manner, yet still on the saving side. I would entertain my self in forming and directing the minds of hopeful young men, by convincing them from my own remembrance, experience and observation, fortified by numerous examples of the usefulness of virtue in publick and private life. But, my choice and constant companions, should be a set of my own immortal brotherhood; among whom I would elect a dozen from the most ancient down to my own contemporaries. Where any of these wanted fortunes, I would provide them with convenient lodges round my own estate, and have some of them always at my table, only mingling a few of the most valuable among you mortals; whom length of time would harden me to lose with little or no reluctance, and treat your posterity after the same manner: just as a man diverts himself with the annual succession of pinks and tulips in his garden, without regretting the loss of those which withered the preceding year.

These Struldbruggs and I would mutually communicate our observations and memorials through the course of time; remark the several gradations by which corruption steals into the world, and oppose it in every step, by giving perpetual warning and instruction to mankind; which, added to the strong influence of our own example, would probably prevent that continual degeneracy of human nature, so justly complained of in all ages.

Add to all this, the pleasure of seeing the various revolutions of states and empires; the changes in the lower and upper world; antient cities in ruins, and obscure villages become the seats of kings. Famous rivers lessening into shallow brooks; the ocean leaving one coast dry, and overwhelming another: the discovery of many countries yet unknown. Barbarity over-running the politest nations, and the most barbarous becoming civilized. I should then see the discovery of the *longitude*, the *perpetual motion*, the *universal medicine*, and many other great inventions brought to the utmost perfection.

What wonderful discoveries should we make in astronomy, by outliving and confirming our own predictions; by observing the progress and returns of comets, with the changes of motion in the sun, moon and stars.

I enlarged upon many other topicks, which the natural desire of endless life and sublunary happiness could easily furnish me with. When I had ended, and the sum of my discourse had been interpreted as before, to the rest of the company, there was a good deal of talk among them in the language of the country, not without some laughter at my expense. At last, the same gentleman who had been my interpeter, said, he was desired by the rest, to set me right in a few mistakes, which I had fallen into through the common imbecility of human nature, and upon that allowance was less answerable for them. That, this breed of Struldbruggs was peculiar to their country, for there were no such people either in Balnibarbi or Japan, where he had the honour to be ambassador from his Majesty, and found the natives in both those kingdoms, very hard to believe that the fact was possible; and it appeared from my astonishment when he first mentioned the matter to me, that I received it as a thing wholly new, and scarcely to be credited. That, in the two kingdoms above-mentioned, where during his residence he had conversed very much, he observed long life to be the universal desire and wish of mankind. That, whoever had one foot in the grave, was sure to hold back the other as strongly as he could. That, the oldest had still hopes of living one day longer, and looked on death as the greatest evil, from which nature always prompted him to retreat; only in this island of Luggnagg, the appetite for living was not so eager, from the continual example of the Struldbruggs before their eyes.

That, the system of living contrived by me was unreasonable and unjust, because it supposed a perpetuity of youth, health, and vigour, which no man could be so foolish to hope, however extravagant he might be in his wishes. That, the question therefore was not whether a man would chuse to be always in the prime of youth, attended with prosperity and health; but how he would pass a perpetual life under all the usual disadvantages which old age brings along with it. For, although few men will avow their desires of being immortal upon such hard conditions, yet in the two kingdoms beforementioned of Balnibarbi and Japan, he observed that every man desired to put off death for some time longer, let it approach ever so late; and he rarely heard of any man who died willingly, except he were excited by the extremity of grief or torture. And he appealed to me whether in those countries I had travelled as well as my own, I had not observed the same general disposition.

After this preface, he gave me a particular account of the Struldbruggs among them. He said they commonly acted like mortals, until about thirty years old, after which by degrees they grew melancholy and dejected, increasing in both until they came to fourscore. This he learned from their own confession; for otherwise, there not being above two or three of that species born in an age, they were too few to form a general observation by. When they came to fourscore years, which is reckoned the extremity of living in this country, they had not only all the follies and infirmities of other old men, but many more which arose from the dreadful prospect of never dying. They were not only opinionative, peevish, covetous, morose, vain, talkative; but uncapable of friendship, and dead to all natural affection, which never descended below their grand-children. Envy and impotent desires, are their prevailing passions. But those objects against which their envy seems principally directed, are the vices of the younger sort, and the deaths of the old. By reflecting on the former, they find themselves cut off from all possibility of pleasure; and whenever they see a funeral, they lament and repine that others are gone to a harbour of rest, to which they themselves never can hope to arrive. They have no remembrance of any thing but what they learned and observed in their youth and middle age, and even that is very imperfect: and for the truth or particulars of any fact, it is safer to depend on common traditions, than upon their best recollections. The least miserable among them, appear to be those who turn to dotage, and entirely lose their memories; these meet with more pity and assistance, because they want many bad qualities which abound in others.

If a Struldbrugg happen to marry one of his own kind, the marriage is dissolved of course by the courtesy of the kingdom, as soon as the younger of the two comes to be fourscore. For the law thinks it a reasonable indulgence, that those who are condemned without any fault of their own, to a perpetual continuance in the world, should not have their misery doubled by the load of a wife.

As soon as they have compleated the term of eighty years, they are looked on as dead in law; their heirs immediately succeed to their estates, only a small pittance is reserved for their support; and the poor ones are maintained at the publick charge. After that period, they are held incapable of any employment of trust or profit; they cannot purchase lands, or take leases; neither are they allowed to be witnesses in any cause, either civil or criminal, not even for the decision of meers and bounds.

At ninety they lose their teeth and hair; they have at that age no distinction of taste, but eat and drink what ever they can get, without relish or appetite. The diseases they were subject to, still continue without encreasing or diminishing. In talking, they forget the common appellation of things, and the names of persons, even of those, who are their nearest friends and relations. For the same reason, they never can amuse themselves with reading, because their memory will not serve to carry them from the beginning of a sentence to the end; and by this defect, they are deprived of the only entertainment whereof they might otherwise be capable.

The language of this country being always upon the flux, the Struldbruggs of one age, do not understand those of another; neither are they able after two hundred years, to hold any conversation (farther than by a few general words) with their neighbours the mortals; and thus they lye under the disadvantage of living like foreigners in their own country.

This was the account given me of the Struldbruggs, as near as I can remember. I afterwards saw five or six of different ages, the youngest not above two hundred years old, who were brought to me at several times by some of my friends; but although they were told that I was a great traveller, and had seen all the world, they had not the least curiosity to ask me a question; only desired I would give them *slumskudask*, or a token of remembrance; which is a modest way of begging, to avoid the law that strictly forbids it, because they are provided for by the publick, although, indeed, with a very scanty allowance.

They are despised and hated by all sorts of people: when one of them is born, it is reckoned ominous, and their birth is recorded very particularly; so that you may know their age by consulting the registry, which however, hath not been kept above a thousand years past, or at least, hath been destroyed by time or publick disturbances. But the usual way of computing how old they are, is, by asking them what kings or great persons they can remember, and then consulting history; for infallibly, the last prince in their mind, did not begin his reign after they were fourscore years old.

They were the most mortifying sight I ever beheld; and the

women more horrible than the men. Besides the usual deformities in extreme old age, they acquired an additional ghastliness in proportion to their number of years, which is not to be described; and among half a dozen I soon distinguished which was the eldest, although there were not above a century or two between them.

The reader will easily believe, that from what I had heard and seen, my keen appetite for perpetuity of life was much abated. I grew heartily ashamed of the pleasing visions I had formed; and thought no tyrant could invent a death into which I would not run with pleasure from such a life. The king heard of all that had passed between me and my friends upon this occasion, and rallied me very pleasantly; wishing I would send a couple of Struldbruggs to my own country, to arm our people against the fear of death; but this it seems is forbidden by the fundamental laws of the kingdom; or else, I should have been well content with the trouble and expence of transporting them.

I could not but agree, that the laws of this kingdom relating to the Struldbruggs, were founded upon the strongest reasons, and such as any other country would be under the necessity of enacting in the like circumstances. Otherwise, as avarice is the necessary consequent of old age, those immortals would in time, become proprietors of the whole nation, and engross the civil power; which, for want of abilities to manage, must end in the ruin of the publick.

NOTES

Alexander the Great (356–323 BC). Arbela, a town east of the River Tigris, gave its name to a great battle fought in October, 331 BC at Gaugamela, fifty miles or so away. Darius of the Persians, with a force estimated at one million men, including 40,000 cavalry, was routed by Alexander's army of about 50,000 men.

Hannibal (247–182 BC) was a Carthaginian who challenged Rome in bitterly fought wars. He decided to march on Rome itself and in 218 BC made his famous crossing of the Alps. The legend that he melted the Alpine rocks with vinegar is thought to have originated in the misunderstanding of a Greek word, which possibly implied some kind of explosive.

Caesar and Pompey. Caesar defeated Pompey in 48 BC at the battle of Pharsalia. Pompey was murdered soon afterwards in Egypt. Caesar was later offered the gift of Pompey's head, but he scorned it and had Pompey's assassins put to death. In 45 BC, after his return from a victorious campaign in Spain, Caesar was loaded with fresh honours by the Senate and made Imperator and Dictator for life. His statue was placed in temples and his image was put on coins; his person was pronounced sacred. He was murdered in 44 BC by the conspirators led by Cassius and Brutus.

Junius. He was the founder of a noble Roman line, the most famous of which was Marcus Junius Brutus (85–42 BC) who murdered Caesar and then took his own life at the battle of Philippi.

Socrates (469–399 BC) was born near Athens, the son of Sophroniscus, a sculptor. He was apparently very uncouth in his appearance and he had a distinguished military career before returning to Athens, where he showed great courage in opposing corruption. His teaching and philosophical discourses are set out in Plato's *Dialogues*. Meletus, a leather-seller, accused Socrates of impiety and the philosopher was condemned to death by drinking hemlock.

Epaminondas was a Theban leader who defeated the Spartans when they invaded Bœotia at the battle of Leuctra (371 BC). Epaminondas went on to attack the Peloponnesus, freeing Arcadian and Messenian vassals from Sparta as he went. In 362 BC, when he had the city of Sparta at his mercy, he was killed at Mantinea, with the result that the Thebans were demoralized and failed to press home their advantage.

Cato, the Younger (95–46 BC) was descended from Cato, the Censor, famous for his opposition to the prevalent luxurious fashions of his time and for his persistent opposition to the Roman government. Cato, the Younger, is remembered for his rigid Stoicism and hostility to Caesar. He committed suicide at Utica after the battle of Thapsus.

Sir Thomas More (1478–1535) was the author of *Utopia* (see the Introduction). He served Henry VIII faithfully and succeeded Wolsey as Lord Chancellor in 1529, but resigned the post in 1532. He refused to swear fidelity to the new Act of Succession and was committed to the Tower, indicted of high treason, condemned, and beheaded in 1535.

The Strange Case of Dr Jekyll and Mr Hyde

R. L. STEVENSON

Robert Louis Stevenson (1850–1894) was educated at Edinburgh University, where he studied engineering before abandoning it for the law. He was called to the Bar in 1875, but never practised. He visited America twice before settling in Samoa, where he died of consumption at the age of forty-four.

The Strange Case of Dr Jekyll and Mr Hyde *was first published in 1886 and had its immediate origin in a dream, it seems. His wife wrote that in the small hours one morning in 1885, 'I was awakened by cries of horror from Louis. Thinking he had a nightmare, I awakened him. He cried angrily, "Why did you wake me? I was dreaming a fine bogey tale."' The first draft of the tale failed to please his wife because of its lack of allegory and so Stevenson burnt it – but he rewrote it three days later. Like Flaubert, Stevenson was a careful stylist who constantly revised his work and only after several more months of work on the story did he release it for publication.*

It is a strange tale which evokes the gaslights and swirling fog of Victorian London, the desperate investigations into science, and the interest at the close of the century into the real nature of mankind. It is an allegory, perhaps, but the moral comment implicit throughout in Jekyll's rejection of Hyde's bestiality is only part of it. It is science which brings about the transformation of the man's nature and it is science which can provide him with relief.

For the reader of science fiction there is a special interest in the story as it is in the tradition of 'Frankenstein' – the irresponsible researcher who cannot control the results of his work and is torn apart from within as a result – but the story is essentially that of Faust – the educated man who strives for knowledge and probes the darkest recesses by science, only to be destroyed by his own art.

This extract forms the conclusion to Stevenson's story. It is in the form of a statement written by Dr Jekyll for his close friend and lawyer, Mr Utterson, who read it only after the body of Edward Hyde had been found in the cabinet of Dr Jekyll. Edward Hyde had committed suicide.

I was born in the year 18— to a large fortune endowed besides with excellent parts, inclined by nature to industry, fond of the respect of the wise and good among my fellowmen, and thus, as might have been supposed, with every guarantee of an honourable and distinguished future. And indeed the worst of my faults was a certain impatient gaiety of disposition, such as has made the happiness of many, but such as I found it hard to reconcile with my imperious desire to carry my head high, and wear a more than commonly grave countenance before the public. Hence it came about that I concealed my pleasures; and that when I reached years of reflection, and began to look round me and take stock of my progress and position in the world, I stood already committed to a profound duplicity of life. Many a man would have even blazoned such irregularities as I was guilty of; but from the high views that I had set before me, I regarded and hid them with an almost morbid sense of shame. It was thus rather the exacting nature of my aspirations than any particular degradation in my faults, that made me what I was, and, with even a deeper trench than in the majority of men, severed in me those provinces of good and ill which divide and compound man's dual nature. In this case, I was driven to reflect deeply and inveterately on that hard law of life, which lies at the root of religion and is one of the most plentiful springs of distress. Though so profound a double-dealer, I was in no sense a hypocrite; both sides of me were in dead earnest; I was no more myself when I laid aside restraint and plunged in shame, than when I laboured, in the eye of day, at the furtherance of knowledge or the relief of sorrow and suffering. And it chanced that the direction of my scientific studies, which led wholly towards the mystic and transcendental, reacted and shed a strong light on this consciousness of the perennial war among my members. With every day, and from both sides of my intelligence, the moral and the intellectual, I thus drew steadily nearer to that truth, by whose partial discovery I have been doomed to such a dreadful shipwreck: that man is not truly one, but truly two. I say two, because the state of my own knowledge does not pass beyond that point. Others will follow, others will outstrip me on the same lines; and I hazard the guess that man will be ultimately known for a mere polity of multifarious, incongruous and independent denizens. I for my part, from the nature of my life, advanced infallibly in one direction and in one direction only. It was on the moral side, and in my own person, that I learned to recognize the thorough and primitive duality of man; I saw that, of the two natures that contended in the field of my consciousness, even if I could rightly be said to be either, it was only because I was radically both; and from an early date, even before the course of my scientific discoveries had begun to suggest the most naked possibility of such a miracle, I had learned to dwell with pleasure, as a beloved day-dream, on the thought of the separation of these elements. If each, I told myself, could but be housed in separate identities, life would be relieved of all that was unbearable; the unjust might go his way, delivered from the aspirations and remorse of his more upright twin; and the just could walk steadfastly and securely on his upward path, doing the good things in which he found his pleasure, and no longer exposed to disgrace and penitence by the hands of this extraneous evil. It was the curse of mankind that these incongruous faggots were thus bound together – that in the agonized womb of consciousness, these polar twins should be continuously struggling. How, then, were they dissociated?

I was so far in my reflections when, as I have said, a side light began to shine upon the subject from the laboratory table. I began to perceive more deeply than it has ever yet been stated, the trembling immateriality, the mist-like transience, of this seemingly so solid body in which we walk attired. Certain agents I found to have the power to shake and to pluck back that fleshly vestment, even as a wind might toss the curtains of a pavilion. For two good reasons, I will not enter deeply into this scientific branch of my confession. First, because I have been made to learn that the doom and burthen of our life is bound forever on man's shoulders, and when the attempt is made to cast it off, it but returns upon us with more unfamiliar and more awful pressure. Second, because, as my narrative will make, alas! too evident, my discoveries were incomplete. Enough, then, that I not only recognized my natural body for the mere aura and effulgence of certain of the powers that made up my spirit, but managed to compound a drug by which these powers should be dethroned from their supremacy, and a second form and countenance substituted, none the less natural to me because they were the expression, and bore the stamp, of lower elements in my soul.

I hesitated long before I put this theory to the test of practice. I knew well that I risked death; for any drug that so potently controlled and shook the very fortress of identity, might by the least scruple of an overdose or at the least inopportunity in the moment of exhibition, utterly blot out the immaterial tabernacle which I looked to it to change. But the temptation of a discovery so singular and profound, at last overcame the suggestions of alarm. I had long since prepared my tincture; I purchased at once, from a firm of wholesale chemists, a large quantity of a particular salt which I knew, from my experiments, to be the last ingredient required; and late one accursed night, I compounded the elements, watched them boil and smoke together in the glass, and when the ebullition had subsided, with a strong glow of courage, drank off the potion.

The most racking pangs succeeded: a grinding in the bones, deadly nausea, and a horror of the spirit that cannot be exceeded at the hour of birth or death. Then these agonies began swiftly to subside, and I came to myself as if out of a great sickness. There was something strange in my sensations, something indescribably new and, from its very novelty, incredibly sweet. I felt younger, lighter, happier in body; within I was conscious of a heady recklessness, a current of disordered sensual images running like a mill race in my fancy, a solution of the bonds of obligation, an unknown but not an innocent freedom of the soul. I knew myself, at the first breath of this new life, to be more wicked, tenfold more wicked, sold a slave to my original evil; and the thought, in that moment, braced and delighted me like wine. I stretched out my hands, exulting in the freshness of these sensations; and in the act, I was suddenly aware that I had lost in stature.

There was no mirror, at that date, in my room; that which stands beside me as I write, was brought there later on and for the very purpose of these transformations. The night, however, was far gone into the morning – the morning, black as it was, was nearly ripe for the conception of the day – the inmates of my house were locked in the most rigorous hours of slumber; and I determined, flushed as I was with hope and triumph, to venture in my new shape as far as to my bedroom. I crossed the yard, wherein the constellations looked down upon me, I could have thought, with wonder, the first creature of that sort that their unsleeping vigilance had yet disclosed to them; I stole through the corridors, a stranger in my own house; and coming to my room, I saw for the first time the appearance of Edward Hyde.

I must here speak by theory alone, saying not that which I know, but that which I suppose to be most probable. The evil side of my nature, to which I had now transferred the stamping efficiency, was less robust and less developed than the good which I had just deposed. Again, in the course of my life, which had been, after all, nine-tenths a life of effort, virtue and control, it had been much less exercised and much less exhausted. And hence, as I think, it came about that Edward Hyde was so much smaller, slighter, and younger than Henry Jekyll. Even as good shone upon the countenance of the one, evil was written broadly and plainly on the face of the other. Evil besides (which I must still believe to be the lethal side of man) had left on that body an imprint of deformity and decay. And yet when I looked upon that ugly idol in the glass, I was conscious of no repugnance, rather of a leap of welcome. This, too, was myself. It seemed natural and human. In my eyes it bore a livelier image of the spirit, it seemed more express and single, than the imperfect and divided countenance I had been hitherto accustomed to call mine. And in so far I was doubtless right. I have observed that when I wore the semblance of Edward Hyde, none could come near to me at first without a visible misgiving of the flesh. This, as I take it, was because all human beings, as we meet them, are commingled out of good and evil: and Edward Hyde, alone in the ranks of mankind, was pure evil.

I lingered but a moment at the mirror: the second and conclusive experiment had yet to be attempted; it yet remained to be seen if I had lost my identity beyond redemption and must flee before daylight from a house that was no longer mine; and hurrying back to my cabinet, I once more prepared and drank the cup, once more suffered the pangs of dissolution, and came to myself once more with the character, the stature and the face of Henry Jekyll.

That night I had come to the fatal cross roads. Had I approached my discovery in a more noble spirit, had I risked the experiment while under the empire of generous or pious aspirations, all must have been otherwise, and from these agonies of death and birth, I had come forth an angel instead of a fiend. The drug had no discriminating action; it was neither diabolical nor divine; it but shook the doors of the prison-house of my disposition; and like the captives of Philippi, that which stood within ran forth. At that time my virtue slumbered; my evil, kept away by ambition, was alert and swift to seize the occasion; and the thing that was projected was Edward Hyde. Hence, although I had now two characters as well as two appearances, one was wholly evil, and the other was still the old Henry Jekyll, that incongruous compound of whose reformation and improvement I had already learned to despair. The movement was thus wholly towards the worse.

Even at that time, I had not yet conquered my aversion to the dryness of a life of study. I would still be merrily disposed at times; and as my pleasures were (to say the least) undignified, and I was not only well known and highly considered, but growing towards the elderly man, this incoherency of my life was daily growing more unwelcome. It was on this side that my new power tempted me until I fell in slavery. I had but to drink the cup, to doff at once the body of the noted professor, and to assume, like a thick cloak, that of Edward Hyde. I smiled at the notion; it seemed to me at the time to be humorous; and I made my preparations with the most studious care. I took and furnished that house in Soho, to which Hyde was tracked by the police; and engaged as housekeeper a creature whom I well knew to be silent and unscrupulous. On the other side, I announced to my servants that a Mr Hyde (whom I described) was to have full liberty and power about my house in the square; and to parry mishaps, I even called and made myself a familiar object, in my second character. I next drew up that will to which you so much objected; so that if anything befell me in the person of Dr Jekyll, I could enter on that of Edward Hyde without pecuniary loss. And thus fortified, as I supposed on every side, I began to profit by the strange immunities of my position.

Men have before hired bravos to transact their crimes, while their own person and reputation sat under shelter. I was the first that ever did so for his pleasures. I was the first that could thus plod in the public eye with a load of genial respectability, and in a moment, like a schoolboy, strip off these lendings and spring headlong into the sea of liberty. But for me, in my impenetrable mantle, the safety was complete. Think of it – I did not even exit! Let me but escape into my laboratory door, give me but a second or two to mix and swallow the draught that I had always standing ready; and whatever he had done, Edward Hyde would pass away like the stain of breath upon a mirror; and there in his stead, quietly at home, trimming the midnight lamp in his study, a man who could afford to laugh at suspicion, would be Henry Jekyll.

The pleasures which I made haste to seek in my disguise were, as I have said, undignified; I would scarce use a harder term. But in the hands of Edward Hyde, they soon began to turn towards the monstrous. When I would come back from these excursions, I was often plunged into a kind of wonder at my vicarious depravity. This familiar that I called out of my soul, and sent forth alone to do his good pleasure, was a being inherently malign and villainous; his every act and thought centered on self; drinking pleasure with bestial avidity from any degree of torture to another; relentless like a man of stone. Henry Jekyll stood at times aghast before the acts of Edward Hyde; but the situation was apart from ordinary laws, and insidiously relaxed the grasp of conscience. It was Hyde, after all, and Hyde alone, that was guilty. Jekyll was no worse; he woke again to his good qualities seemingly unimpaired; he would even make haste, where it was possible, to undo the evil done by Hyde. And thus his conscience slumbered.

Into the details of the infamy at which I thus connived (for even now I can scarce grant that I committed it) I have no design of entering; I mean but to point out the warnings and the successive steps with which my chastisement approached. I met with one accident which, as it brought on no consequence, I shall no more than mention. An act of cruelty to a child aroused against me the anger of a passer-by, whom I recognized the other day in the person of your kinsman; the doctor and the child's family joined him; there were moments when I feared for my life; and at last, in order to pacify their too just resentment, Edward Hyde had to bring them to the door, and pay them in a cheque drawn in the name of Henry Jekyll. But this danger was easily eliminated from the future, by opening an account at another bank in the name of Edward Hyde himself; and when, by sloping my own hand backward, I had supplied my double with a signature, I thought I sat beyond the reach of fate.

Some two months before the murder of Sir Danvers, I had been out for one of my adventures, had returned at a late hour, and woke the next day in bed, with somewhat odd sensations. It was in vain I looked about me; in vain I saw the decent furniture and tall proportions of my room in the square; in vain that I recognized the pattern of the bed curtains and the design of the mahogany frame; something still kept insisting that I was not where I was, that I had not wakened where I seemed to be, but in the little room in Soho where I was accustomed to sleep in the body of Edward Hyde. I smiled to myself, and, in my psychological way began lazily to inquire into the elements of this illusion, occasionally, even as I did so, dropping back into a comfortable morning doze. I was still so engaged when, in one of my more wakeful moments, my eyes fell upon my hand. Now the hand of Henry Jekyll (as you have often remarked) was professional in shape and size: it was large, firm, white and comely. But the hand which I now saw, clearly enough, in the yellow light of a mid-London morning, lying half shut on the bed clothes, was lean, corded, knuckly, of a dusky pallor and thickly shaded with a swart growth of hair. It was the hand of Edward Hyde.

I must have stared upon it for near half a minute, sunk as I was in the mere stupidity of wonder, before terror woke up in my breast as sudden and startling as the crash of cymbals; and bounding from my bed, I rushed to the mirror. At the sight that met my eyes, my blood was changed into something exquisitely thin and icy. Yes, I had gone to bed Henry Jekyll, I had awakened Edward Hyde. How was this to be explained I asked myself; and then, with another bound of terror – how was it to be remedied? It was well on in the morning; the servants were up; all my drugs were in the cabinet – a long journey down two pair of stairs, through the back passage, across the open court and through the anatomical theatre, from where I was then standing horror-struck. It might indeed be possible to cover my face; but of what use was that, when I was unable to conceal the alteration in my stature? And then with an overpowering sweetness of relief, it came back upon my mind that the servants were already used to the coming and going of my second self. I had soon dressed, as well as I was able, in clothes of my own size: had soon passed through the house, where Bradshaw stared and drew back at seeing Mr Hyde at such an hour and in such a strange array; and ten minutes later, Dr Jekyll had returned to his own shape and was sitting down, with a darkened brow, to make a feint of breakfasting.

Small indeed was my appetite. This inexplicable incident, this reversal of my previous experience, seemed, like the Babylonian finger on the wall, to be spelling out the letters of my judgment; and I began to reflect more seriously than ever before on the issues and possibilities of my double existence. That part of me which I had the power of projecting, had lately been much exercised and nourished; it had seemed to me of late as though the body of Edward Hyde had grown in stature, as though (when I wore that form) I were conscious of a more generous tide of blood; and I began to spy a danger that, if this were much prolonged, the balance of my nature might be permanently overthrown, the power of voluntary change be forfeited, and the character of Edward Hyde become irrevocably mine. The power of the drug had not been always equally displayed. Once, very early in my career, it had totally failed me; since then I had been obliged on more than one occasion to double, and once, with infinite risk of death, to treble the amount; and these rare uncertainties had cast hitherto the sole shadow on my contentment. Now, however, and in the light of that morning's accident, I was led to remark that whereas, in the beginning, the difficulty had been to throw off the body of Jekyll, it had of late gradually but decidedly transferred itself to the other side. All things therefore seemed to point to this: that I was slowly losing hold of my original and better self, and becoming slowly incorporated with my second and worse.

Between these two, I now felt I had to choose. My two natures had memory in common, but all other faculties were most unequally shared between them. Jekyll (who was composite) now with the most sensitive apprehensions, now with a greedy gusto, projected and shared in the pleasures and adventures of Hyde; but Hyde was indifferent to Jekyll, or but remembered him as the mountain bandit remembers the cavern in which he conceals himself from pursuit. Jekyll had more than a father's interest; Hyde had more than a son's indifference. To cast in my lot with Jekyll, was to die to those appetites which I had long secretly indulged and had of late begun to pamper. To cast it in with Hyde, was to die to a thousand interests and aspirations, and to become, at a blow and forever, despised and friendless. The bargain might appear unequal; but there was still another consideration in the scales; for while Jekyll would suffer smartingly in the fires of abstinence, Hyde would not be even conscious of all that he had lost. Strange as my circumstances were, the terms of this debate are as old and commonplace as man; much the same inducements and alarms cast the die for any tempted and trembling sinner; and it fell out with me, as it falls with so vast a majority of my fellows, that I chose the better part and was found wanting in the strength to keep to it.

Yes, I preferred the elderly and discontented doctor, surrounded by friends and cherishing honest hopes; and bade a resolute farewell to the liberty, the comparative youth, the light step, leaping impulses and secret pleasures, that I had enjoyed in the disguise of Hyde. I made this choice perhaps with some unconscious reservation, for I neither gave up the house in Soho, nor destroyed the clothes of Edward Hyde, which still lay ready in my cabinet. For two months, however, I was true to my determination; for two months I led a life of such severity as I had never before attained to, and enjoyed the compensations of an approving conscience. But time began at last to obliterate the freshness of my alarm; the praises of conscience began to grow into a thing of course; I began to be tortured with throes and longings, as of Hyde struggling after freedom; and at last, in an hour of moral weakness, I once again compounded and swallowed the transforming draught.

I do not suppose that, when a drunkard reasons with himself upon his vice, he is once out of five hundred times affected by the dangers that he runs through his brutish, physical insensibility; neither had I, long as I had considered my position, made enough allowance for the complete moral insensibility and insensate readiness to evil, which were the leading characters of Edward Hyde. Yet it was by these that I was punished. My devil had been long caged; he came out roaring. I was conscious, even when I took the draught, of a more unbridled, a more furious propensity to ill. It must have been this, I suppose, that stirred in my soul that tempest of impatience with which I listened to the civilities of my unhappy victim; I declare, at least, before God, no man morally sane could have been guilty of that crime upon so pitiful a provocation; and that I struck in no more reasonable spirit than that in which a sick child may break a plaything. But I had voluntarily stripped myself of all those balancing instincts by which event the worst of us continues to walk with some degree of steadiness among temptations; and in my case, to be tempted, however slightly, was to fall.

Instantly the spirit of hell awoke in me and raged. With a transport of glee, I mauled the unresisting body, tasting delight from every blow; and it was not till weariness had begun to succeed, that I was suddenly, in the top fit of my delirium, struck through the heart by a cold thrill of terror. A mist dispersed; I saw my life to be forfeit; and fled from the scene of these excesses, at once glorifying and trembling, my lust of evil gratified and stimulated, my love of life screwed to the topmost peg. I ran to the house in Soho, and (to make assurance doubly sure) destroyed my papers; thence I set out through the lamplit streets, in the same divided ecstasy of mind, gloating on my crime, light-headedly devising others in the future, and yet still hastening and still hearkening in my wake for the steps of the avenger. Hyde had a song upon his lips as he compounded the draught, and as he drank it, pledged the dead man. The pangs of transformation had not done tearing him, before Henry Jekyll, with streaming tears of gratitude and remorse, had fallen upon his knees and lifted his clasped hands to God. The veil of self-indulgence was rent from head to foot. I saw my life as a whole: I followed it up from the days of childhood, when I had walked with my father's hand, and through the self-denying toils of my professional life, to arrive again and again, with the same sense of unreality, at the damned horrors of the evening. I could have screamed aloud; I sought with tears and prayers to smother down the crowd of hideous images and sounds with which my memory swarmed against me; and still, between the petitions, the ugly face of my iniquity stared into my soul. As the acuteness of this remorse began to die away, it was succeeded by a sense of joy. The problem of my conduct was solved. Hyde was thenceforth impossible; whether I would or not, I was now confined to the better part of my existence; and O, how I rejoiced to think it! with what willing humility, I embraced anew the restrictions of natural life! with what sincere renunciation, I locked the door by which I had so often gone and come, and ground the key under my heel!

The next day, came the news that the murder had been overlooked,* that the guilt of Hyde was patent to the world, and that the victim was a man high in public estimation. It was not only a crime, it had been a tragic folly. I think I was glad to know it; I think I was glad to have my better impulses thus buttressed and guarded by the terrors of the scaffold. Jekyll was now my city of refuge; let Hyde peep out an instant, and the hands of all men would be raised to take and slay him.

I resolved in my future conduct to redeem the past; and I can say with honesty that my resolve was fruitful of some good. You know yourself how earnestly in the last months of last year, I laboured to relieve suffering; you know that much was done for others, and that the days passed quietly, almost happily for myself. Nor can I truly say that I wearied of this beneficent and innocent life; I think instead that I daily enjoyed it more completely; but I was still cursed with my duality of purpose; and as the first edge of my penitence wore off, the lower side of me, so long indulged, so recently chained down, began to growl for licence. Not that I dreamed of resuscitating Hyde; the bare idea of that would startle me to frenzy: no, it was in my own person, that I was once more tempted to trifle with my conscience; and it was as an ordinary secret sinner that I at last fell before the assaults of temptation.

There comes an end to all things; the most capacious measure is

* A maid-servant had seen Hyde club Sir Danvers Carew to death with a heavy cane.

filled at last; and this brief condescension to my evil finally destroyed the balance of my soul. And yet I was not alarmed; the fall seemed natural, like a return to the old days before I had made my discovery. It was a fine, clear, January day, wet under foot where the frost had melted, but cloudless overhead; and the Regent's Park was full of winter chirrupings and sweet with spring odours. I sat in the sun on a bench; the animal within me licking the chops of memory; the spiritual side a little drowsed, promising subsequent penitence, but not yet moved to begin. After all, I reflected, I was like my neighbours; and then I smiled, comparing myself with other men, comparing my active goodwill with the lazy cruelty of their neglect. And at the very moment of that vain-glorious thought, a qualm came over me, a horrid nausea and the most deadly shuddering. These passed away, and left me faint; and then as in its turn the faintness subsided, I began to be aware of a change in the temper of my thoughts, a greater boldness, a contempt of danger, a solution of the bonds of obligation. I looked down; my clothes hung formlessly on my shrunken limbs; the hand that lay on my knee was corded and hairy. I was once more Edward Hyde. A moment before I had been safe of all men's respect, wealthy, beloved – the cloth lying for me in the dining-room at home; and now I was the common quarry of mankind, hunted, houseless, a known murderer, thrall to the gallows.

My reason wavered, but it did not fail me utterly. I have more than once observed that, in my second character, my faculties seemed sharpened to a point and my spirits more tensely elastic; thus it came about that, where Jekyll perhaps might have succumbed, Hyde rose to the importance of the moment. My drugs were in one of the presses of my cabinet; how was I to reach them? That was the problem that (crushing my temples in my hands) I set myself to solve. The laboratory door I had closed. If I sought to enter by the house, my own servants would consign me to the gallows. I saw I must employ another hand, and thought of Lanyon.* How was he to be reached? how persuaded? Supposing that I escaped capture in the streets, how was I to make my way into his presence? and how should I, an unknown and displeasing visitor, prevail on the famous physician to rifle the study of his colleague, Dr Jekyll? Then I remembered that of my original character, one part remained to me: I could write my own hand; and once I had conceived that kindling spark, the way that I must follow became lighted up from end to end.

* **Lanyon: his friend and fellow-doctor.**

Thereupon, I arranged my clothes as best I could, and summoning a passing hansom, drove to an hotel in Portland Street, the name of which I chanced to remember. At my appearance (which was indeed comical enough, however tragic a fate these garments covered) the driver could not conceal his mirth. I gnashed my teeth upon him with a gust of devilish fury; and the smile withered from his face – happily for him – yet more happily for myself, for in another instant I had certainly dragged him from his perch. At the inn, as I entered, I looked about me with so black a countenance as made the attendants tremble; not a look did they exchange in my presence; but obsequiously took my orders, led me to a private room, and brought me wherewithal to write. Hyde in danger of his life was a creature new to me; shaken with inordinate anger, strung to the pitch of murder, lusting to inflict pain. Yet the creature was astute; mastered his fury with a great effort of the will; composed his two important letters, one to Lanyon and one to Poole,* and that he might receive actual evidence of their being posted, sent them out with directions that they should be registered.

Thenceforward, he sat all day over the fire in the private room, gnawing his nails; there he dined, sitting alone with his fears, the waiter visibly quailing before his eye; and thence, when the night was fully come, he set forth in the corner of a closed cab, and was driven to and fro about the streets of the city. He, I say – I cannot say, I. That child of Hell had nothing human; nothing lived in him but fear and hatred. And when at last, thinking the driver had begun to grow suspicious, he discharged the cab and ventured on foot, attired in his misfitting clothes, an object marked out for observation, in to the midst of the nocturnal passengers, these two base passions raged within him like a tempest. He walked fast, hunted by his fears, chattering to himself, skulking through the less frequented thoroughfares, counting the minutes that still divided him from midnight. Once a woman spoke to him, offering, I think, a box of lights. He smote her in the face, and she fled.

When I came to myself at Lanyon's, the horror of my old friend perhaps affected me somewhat: I do not know; it was at least but a drop in the sea to the abhorrence with which I looked back upon these hours. A change had come over me. It was no longer the fear of the gallows, it was the horror of being Hyde that racked me. I received Lanyon's condemnation partly in a dream; it was partly in a dream that I came home to my own house and got

* Poole: an elderly servant.

into bed. I slept after the prostration of the day, with a stringent and profound slumber which not even the nightmares that wrung me could avail to break. I awoke in the morning shaken, weakened, but refreshed. I still hated and feared the thought of the brute that slept within me, and I had not of course forgotten the appalling dangers of the day before; but I was once more at home, in my own house and close to my drugs; and gratitude for my escape shone so strong in my soul that it almost rivalled the brightness of hope.

I was stepping leisurely across the court after breakfast, drinking the chill of the air with pleasure, when I was seized again with those indescribable sensations that heralded my change; and I had but the time to gain the shelter of my cabinet, before I was once again raging and freezing with the passions of Hyde. It took on this occasion a double dose to recall me to myself; and alas! six hours after, as I sat looking sadly in the fire, the pangs returned, and the drug had to be readministered. In short, from that day forth it seemed only by a great effort as of gymnastics, and only under the immediate stimulation of the drug, that I was able to wear the countenance of Jekyll. At all hours of the day and night, I would be taken with the premonitory shudder; above all, if I slept, or even dozed for a moment in my chair, it was always as Hyde that I awakened. Under the strain of this continually impending doom and by the sleeplessness to which I now condemned myself, ay, even beyond what I had thought possible to man, I became, in my own person, a creature eaten up and emptied by fever, languidly weak both in body and mind, and solely occupied by one thought: the horror of my other self. But when I slept, or when the virtue of the medicine wore off, I would leap almost without transition (for the pangs of transformation grew daily less marked) into the possession of a fancy brimming with images of terror, a soul boiling with causeless hatreds, and a body that seemed not strong enough to contain the raging energies of life. The powers of Hyde seemed to have grown with the sickliness of Jekyll. And certainly the hate that now divided them was equal on each side. With Jekyll, it was a thing of vital instinct. He had now seen the full deformity of that creature that shared with him some of the phenomena of consciousness, and was co-heir with him to death: and beyond these links of community, which in themselves made the most poignant part of his distress, he thought of Hyde, for all his energy of life, as of something not only hellish but inorganic. This was the shocking thing; that the slime of the pit seemed to utter cries and voices; that the amorphous dust gesticulated and sinned; that what was dead, and had no shape, should usurp the offices of life. And this again, that that insurgent horror was knit to him closer than a wife, closer than an eye; lay caged in his flesh, where he heard it mutter and felt it struggle to be born; and at every hour of weakness, and in the confidence of slumber, prevailed against him, and deposed him out of life. The hatred of Hyde for Jekyll, was of a different order. His terror of the gallows drove him continually to commit temporary suicide, and return to his subordinate station of a part instead of a person; but he loathed the necessity, he loathed the despondency into which Jekyll was now fallen, and he resented the dislike with which he was himself regarded. Hence the apelike tricks that he would play me, scrawling in my own hand blasphemies on the pages of my books, burning the letters and destroying the portrait of my father; and indeed, had it not been for his fear of death, he would long ago have ruined himself in order to involve me in the ruin. But his love of life is wonderful; I go further: I, who sicken and freeze at the mere thought of him, when I recall the abjection and passion of this attachment, and when I know how he fears my power to cut him off by suicide, I find it in my heart to pity him.

It is useless, and the time awfully fails me, to prolong this description; no one has ever suffered such torments, let that suffice; and yet even to these, habit brought – no, not alleviation – but a certain callousness of soul, a certain acquiescence of despair; and my punishment might have gone on for years, but for the last calamity which has now fallen, and which has finally severed me from my own face and nature. My provision of the salt, which had never been renewed since the date of the first experiment, began to run low. I sent out for a fresh supply, and mixed the draught; the ebullition followed, and the first change of colour, not the second; I drank it and it was without efficiency. You will learn from Poole how I have had London ransacked; it was in vain; and I am now persuaded that my first supply was impure, and that it was that unknown impurity which lent efficacy to the draught.

About a week had passed, and I am now finishing this statement under the influence of the last of the old powders. This, then, is the last time, short of a miracle, that Henry Jekyll can think his own thoughts or see his own face (now how sadly altered!) in the glass. Nor must I delay too long to bring my writing to an end; for if my narrative has hitherto escaped destruction, it has been by a combination of great prudence and great good luck. Should the throes of change take me in the act of writing it, Hyde will tear it in pieces; but if some time shall have elapsed after I have laid it by, his wonderful selfishness and circumscription to the moment will probably save it once again from the action of his apelike spite. And indeed the doom that is closing on us both, has already changed and crushed him. Half an hour from now when I shall again and forever reindue that hated personality, I know how I shall sit shuddering and weeping in my chair, or continue, with the most strained and fearstruck ecstasy of listening, to pace up and down this room (my last earthly refuge) and give ear to every sound of menace. Will Hyde die upon the scaffold? or will he find courage to release himself at the last moment? God knows; I am careless; this is my true hour of death, and what is to follow concerns another than myself. Here then, as I lay down the pen and proceed to seal up my confession, I bring the life of that unhappy Henry Jekyll to an end.

In the Abyss

H. G. WELLS

H. G. Wells (1866–1946) was the son of a professional cricketer and a small tradesman. He later became a teacher at Midhurst Grammar School and subsequently studied science at the Normal School of Science in South Kensington, where he took a degree of the University of London.

In the Abyss *was first published in January, 1896, in* Pearson's Magazine *and is of particular interest in the history of the development of science fiction for at least three reasons.*

First, in contrast with a technique often employed by Jules Verne, science is used to get the story under way rather than as the fundamental basis for it. The lieutenant begins the story with an account of water pressure, but in spite of his facility in mental arithmetic he is not allowed by Steevens to bore the reader: 'Sounds a lot . . . but it's jolly thick steel.' Phrases are rapidly tossed into the narrative to give an air of scientific respectability – 'the Myer's apparatus', 'carbonic acid', 'high-pressure water' – but the general reader's attention is kept by homely comparisons – 'like butter over bread', 'like a soda-water bubble'. The scientific details are not crucial to the story, which is just as well, for what effect on a man does a five-mile descent in less than a minute have on his body? What of the sudden rush upwards of the steel sphere when the cable is cut? Are there no problems of decompression? The commander speaks for us all when he says, 'I'm no slavish believer in calculations'; but perhaps not quite for 'all': the purist science fiction reader insists that the science must be complete and accurate. H. G. Wells is content to use the science for the sake of the narrative rather than as an end in itself.

Second, the story exemplifies the early use of 'the bug-eyed monster', now so prominent in science fiction:

> *'It was a biped; its almost globular body was poised on a tripod of two frog-like legs and a long thick tail, and its fore limbs, which grotesquely caricatured the human hand, much as a frog's do, carried a long shaft of bone, tipped with copper. The colour of the*

> *creature was variegated; its head, hands, and legs were purple; but its skin, which hung loosely upon it, even as clothes might do, was a phosphorescent grey. And it stood there blinded by the light.'*

This is the monster alien, menacing in its partly human form. Wells gives a similar description of a Martian in The War of the Worlds, *where the mouth is V-shaped, there is no chin, clusters of tentacles hang down, and the skin is oily and 'fungoid'.* A. E. Vogt's *story* Voyage of the Space Beagle *abounds with such accounts.*

Third, this exploration into 'the unsuspected cities of the deep sea' sets out the reactions of an alien people to man's arrival; what would be man's reaction if an alien people arrived in his world? H. G. Wells poses the problem clearly:

> *'One can understand, perhaps, something of their behaviour at the descent of a living man, if one thinks what a barbaric people might do, to whom an enhaloed, shining creature came suddenly out of the sky.'*

A problem to provoke a thousand stories in the twentieth century, and yet In the Abyss *was published in 1896!*

The lieutenant stood in front of the steel sphere and gnawed a piece of pine splinter. 'What do you think of it, Steevens?' he asked.

'It's an idea,' said Steevens, in the tone of one who keeps an open mind.

'I believe it will smash—flat,' said the lieutenant.

'He seems to have calculated it all out pretty well,' said Steevens, still impartial.

'But think of the pressure,' said the lieutenant. 'At the surface of the water it's fourteen pounds to the inch, thirty feet down it's double that; sixty, treble; ninety, four times; nine hundred, forty times; five thousand, three hundred – that's a mile – it's two hundred and forty times fourteen pounds; that's – let's see – thirty hundred-weight – a ton and a half, Steevens; *a ton and a half* to the square inch. And the ocean where he's going is five miles deep. That's seven and a half—'

'Sounds a lot,' said Steevens, 'but it's jolly thick steel.'

The lieutenant made no answer, but resumed his pine splinter. The object of their conversation was a huge ball of steel, having an exterior diameter of perhaps nine feet. It looked like the shot for some Titanic piece of artillery. It was elaborately nested in a monstrous scaffolding built into the framework of the vessel, and the gigantic spars that were presently to sling it overboard gave the stern of the ship an appearance that had raised the curiosity of every decent sailor who had sighted it, from the Pool of London to the Tropic of Capricorn. In two places, one above the other, the steel gave place to a couple of circular windows of enormously thick glass, and one of these, set in a steel frame of great solidity, was now partially unscrewed. Both the men had seen the interior of this globe for the first time that morning. It was elaborately padded with air cushions, with little studs sunk between bulging pillows to work the simple mechanism of the affair. Everything was elaborately padded, even the Myer's apparatus which was to absorb carbonic acid and replace the oxygen inspired by its tenant, when he had crept in by the glass manhole, and had been screwed in. It was so elaborately padded that a man might have been fired from a gun in it with perfect safety. And it had needed to be, for presently a man was to crawl in through that glass manhole, to be screwed up tightly, and to be flung overboard, and to sink down – down – down, for five miles, even as the lieutenant said. It had taken the strongest hold of his imagination; it made him a bore at mess; and he found Steevens, the new arrival aboard, a godsend to talk to about it, over and over again.

'It's my opinion,' said the lieutenant, 'that that glass will simply bend in and bulge and smash, under a pressure of that sort. Daubrée has made rocks run like water under big pressures – and, you mark my words—'

'If the glass did break in,' said Steevens, 'what then?'

'The water would shoot in like a jet of iron. Have you ever felt a straight jet of high-pressure water? It would hit as hard as a bullet. It would simply smash him and flatten him. It would tear down his throat, and into his lungs; it would blow in his ears—'

'What a detailed imagination you have!' protested Steevens, who saw things vividly.

'It's a simple statement of the inevitable,' said the lieutenant.

'And the globe?'

'Would just give out a few little bubbles, and it would settle down comfortably against the day of judgement, among the oozes and the bottom clay – with poor Elstead spread over his own smashed cushions like butter over bread.'

He repeated this sentence as though he liked it very much. 'Like butter over bread,' he said.

'Having a look at the jigger?' said a voice, and Elstead stood between them, spick and span in white, with a cigarette between his teeth, and his eyes smiling out of the shadow of his ample hat-brim. 'What's that about bread and butter, Weybridge? Grumbling as usual about the insufficient pay of naval officers? It won't be more than a day now before I start. We are to get the slings ready today. This clean sky and gentle swell is just the kind of thing for swinging off a dozen tons of lead and iron, isn't it?'

'It won't affect you much,' said Weybridge.

'No. Seventy or eighty feet down, and I shall be there in a dozen seconds, there's not a particle moving, though the wind shriek itself hoarse up above, and the water lifts half-way to the clouds. No. Down there—' He moved to the side of the ship and the other two followed him. All three leant forward on their elbows and stared down into the yellow-green water.

'*Peace*,' said Elstead, finishing his thought aloud.

'Are you dead certain that clockwork will act?' asked Weybridge presently.

'It has worked thirty-five times,' said Elstead. 'It's bound to work.'

'But if it doesn't?'

'Why shouldn't it?'

'I wouldn't go down in that confounded thing,' said Weybridge, 'for twenty thousand pounds.'

'Cheerful chap you are,' said Elstead, and spat sociably at a bubble below.

'I don't understand yet how you mean to work the thing,' said Steevens.

'In the first place, I'm screwed into the sphere,' said Elstead, 'and when I've turned the electric light off and on three times to show I'm cheerful, I'm slung out over the stern by that crane, with all those big lead sinkers slung below me. The top lead weight has a roller carrying a hundred fathoms of strong cord rolled up, and that's all that joins the sinkers to the sphere, except the slings that will be cut when the affair is dropped. We use cord rather than wire rope because it's easier to cut and more buoyant – necessary points, as you will see.

'Through each of these lead weights you notice there is a hole, and an iron rod will be run through that and will project six feet on the lower side. If that rod is rammed up from below, it knocks up a lever and sets the clockwork in motion at the side of the cylinder on which the cord winds.

'Very well. The whole affair is lowered gently into the water, and the slings are cut. The sphere floats – with the air in it, it's lighter than water – but the lead weights go down straight and the cord runs out. When the cord is all paid out, the sphere will go down too, pulled down by the cord.'

'But why the cord?' asked Steevens. 'Why not fasten the weights directly to the sphere?'

'Because of the smash down below. The whole affair will go rushing down, mile after mile, at a headlong pace at last. It would be knocked to pieces on the bottom if it wasn't for that cord. But the weights will hit the bottom, and directly they do the buoyancy of the sphere will come into play. It will go on sinking slower and slower; come to a stop at last, and then begin to float upward again.

'That's where the clockwork comes in. Directly the weights smash against the sea bottom, the rod will be knocked through and will kick up the clockwork, and the cord will be rewound on the reel. I shall be lugged down to the sea bottom. There I shall stay for half an hour, with the electric light on, looking about me. Then the clockwork will release a spring knife, the cord will be cut, and up I shall rush again, like a soda-water bubble. The cord itself will help the flotation.'

'And if you should chance to hit a ship?' said Weybridge.

'I should come up at such a pace, I should go clean through it,' said Elstead, 'like a cannon-ball. You needn't worry about that.'

'And suppose some nimble crustacean should wriggle into your clockwork—'

'It would be a pressing sort of invitation for me to stop,' said Elstead, turning his back on the water and staring at the sphere.

They had swung Elstead overboard by eleven o'clock. The day was serenely bright and calm, with the horizon lost in haze. The electric glare in the little upper compartment beamed cheerfully three times. Then they let him down slowly to the surface of the water, and a sailor in the stern chains hung ready to cut the tackle that held the lead weights and the sphere together. The globe, which had looked so large on deck, looked the smallest thing conceivable under the stern of the ship. It rolled a little, and its two dark windows, which floated uppermost, seemed like eyes turned up in round wonderment at the people who crowded the rail. A voice wondered how Elstead liked the rolling. 'Are you ready?' sang out the commander. 'Ay, Ay, sir!' 'Then let her go!'

The rope of the tackle tightened against the blade and was cut, and an eddy rolled over the globe in a grotesquely helpless fashion. Someone waved a handkerchief, someone else tried an ineffectual cheer, a middy was counting slowly. 'Eight, nine, ten!' Another roll, then with a jerk and a splash the thing righted itself.

It seemed to be stationary for a moment, to grow rapidly smaller, and then the water closed over it, and it became visible, enlarged by refraction and dimmer, below the surface. Before one could count three it had disappeared. There was a flicker of white light far down in the water, that diminished to a speck and vanished. Then there was nothing but a depth of water going down into blackness, through which a shark was swimming.

Then suddenly the screw of the cruiser began to rotate, the water was crickled, the shark disappeared in a wrinkled confusion, and a torrent of foam rushed across the crystalline clearness that had swallowed up Elstead. 'What's the idea?' said one AB to another.

'We're going to lay off about a couple of miles, 'fear he should hit us when he comes up,' said his mate.

The ship steamed slowly to her new position. Aboard her almost everyone who was unoccupied remained watching the breathing swell into which the sphere had sunk. For the next half-hour it is doubtful if a word was spoken that did not bear directly or indirectly on Elstead. The December sun was now high in the sky, and the heat very considerable.

'He'll be cold enough down there,' said Weybridge. 'They say that below a certain depth sea water's always just about freezing.'

'Where'll he come up?' asked Steevens. 'I've lost my bearings.'

'That's the spot,' said the commander, who prided himself on his omniscience. He extended a precise finger south-eastward. 'And this, I reckon, is pretty nearly the moment,' he said. 'He's been thirty-five minutes.'

'How long does it take to reach the bottom of the ocean?' asked Steevens.

'For a depth of five miles, and reckoning – as we did – an acceleration of two feet per second, both ways, is just about three-quarters of a minute.'

'Then he's overdue,' said Weybridge.

'Pretty nearly,' said the commander. 'I suppose it takes a few minutes for the cord of his to wind in.'

'I forgot that,' said Weybridge, evidently relieved.

And then began the suspense. A minute slowly dragged itself out, and no sphere shot out of the water. Another followed, and nothing broke the low oily swell. The sailors explained to one another that little point about the winding-in of the cord. The rigging was dotted with expectant faces. 'Come up, Elstead!' called one hairy-chested salt, impatiently, and the others caught it up, and shouted as though they were waiting for the curtain of a theatre to rise.

The commander glanced irritably at them.

'Of course, if the acceleration's less than two,' he said, 'he'll be all the longer. We aren't absolutely certain that was the proper figure. I'm no slavish believer in calculations.'

Steevens agreed concisely. No one on the quarter-deck spoke for a couple of minutes. Then Steevens's watchcase clicked.

When, twenty-one minutes after the sun reached the zenith, they were still waiting for the globe to reappear, not a man aboard had dared to whisper that hope was dead. It was Weybridge who first gave expression to that realization. He spoke while the sound of eight bells still hung in the air. 'I always distrusted that window,' he said quite suddenly to Steevens.

'Well!' said Steevens; 'you don't think—'

'Well!' said Weybridge, and left the rest to his imagination.

'I'm no great believer in calculations myself,' said the commander dubiously, 'so that I'm not altogether hopeless yet.' And at midnight the gunboat was steaming slowly in a spiral round the spot where the globe had sunk, and the white beam of the electric light fled and halted and swept discontentedly onward again over the waste of phosphorescent waters under the little stars.

'If his window hasn't burst and smashed him,' said Weybridge, 'then it's a cursed sight worse, for his clockwork has gone wrong, and he's alive now, five miles under our feet, down there in the cold and dark, anchored in that little bubble of his, where never a ray of light has shone or a human being lived, since the waters were gathered together. He's there without food, feeling hungry and thirsty and scared, wondering whether he'll starve or stifle. Which will it be? The Myer's apparatus is running out, I suppose. How long do they last?

'Good heavens!' he exclaimed, 'what little things we are! We daring little devils! Down there, miles and miles of water – all water, and all this empty water about us and this sky. Gulfs!' He threw his hands out, and as he did so, a little white streak swept noiselessly up the sky, travelled more slowly, stopped, became a motionless dot, as though a new star had fallen up into the sky. Then it went sliding back again and lost itself amidst the reflections of the stars and the white haze of the sea's phosphorescence.

At the sight he stopped, arm extended and mouth open. He shut his mouth, opened it again, and waved his arms with an impatient gesture. Then he turned, shouted 'El-stead ahoy!' to the first watch, and went at a run to Lindley and the search-light. 'I saw him!' he said. 'Starboard there! His light's on, and he's just shot out of the water. Bring the light round. We ought to see him drifting, when he lifts on the swell.'

But they never picked up the explorer until dawn. Then they almost ran him down. The crane was swung out and a boat's crew hooked the chain to the sphere. When they had shipped the sphere, they unscrewed the manhole and peered into the darkness of the interior (for the electric light chamber was intended to illuminate the water about the sphere, and was shut off entirely from its general cavity).

The air was very hot within the cavity, and the india-rubber at the lip of the manhole was soft. There was no answer to their eager questions and no sound of movement within. Elstead seemed to be lying motionless, crumpled up in the bottom of the globe. The ship's doctor crawled in and lifted him out to the men outside. For a moment or so they did not know whether Elstead was alive or dead. His face, in the yellow light of the ship's lamps, glistened with perspiration. They carried him down to his own cabin.

He was not dead, they found, but in a state of absolute nervous collapse, and besides cruelly bruised. For some days he had to lie perfectly still. It was a week before he could tell his experiences.

Almost his first words were that he was going down again. The sphere would have to be altered, he said, in order to allow him to throw off the cord if need be, and that was all. He had had the most marvellous experience. 'You thought I should find nothing but ooze,' he said. 'You laughed at my explorations, and I've discovered a new world!' He told his story in disconnected fragments, and chiefly from the wrong end, so that it is impossible to re-tell it in his words. But what follows is the narrative of his experience.

It began atrociously, he said. Before the cord ran out, the thing kept rolling over. He felt like a frog in a football. He could see nothing but the crane of the sky overhead, with an occasional glimpse of the people on the ship's rail. He couldn't tell a bit which way the thing would roll next. Suddenly he would find his feet going up, and try to step, and over he went rolling, head over heels, and just anyhow, on the padding. Any other shape would have been more comfortable, but no other shape was to be relied upon under the huge pressure of the nethermost abyss.

Suddenly the swaying ceased, the globe righted, and when he had picked himself up, he saw the water all about him greeny-blue, with an attenuated light filtering down from above, and a shoal of little floating things went rushing up past him, as it seemed to him, towards the light. And even as he looked, it grew darker and darker, until the water above was as dark as the midnight sky, albeit of a greener shade, and the water below black. And little transparent things in the water developed a faint glint of luminosity, and shot past him in faint greenish streaks.

And the feeling of falling! It was just like the start of a lift, he said, only it kept on. One has to imagine what that means, that keeping on. It was then of all times that Elstead repented of his adventure. He saw the chances against him in an altogether new light. He thought of the big cuttle-fish people knew to exist in the middle waters, the kind of things they find half digested in whales at times, or floating dead and rotten and half eaten by fish. Suppose one caught hold and wouldn't let go. And had the clockwork really been sufficiently tested? But whether he wanted to go on or back mattered not the slightest now.

In fifty seconds everything was as black as night outside, except where the beam from his light struck through the waters, and picked out every now and then some fish or scrap of sinking matter. They flashed by too fast for him to see what they were. Once he thinks he passed a shark. And then the sphere began to get hot by friction against the water. They had under-estimated this, it seems.

The first thing he noticed was that he was perspiring, and then he heard a hissing growing louder under his feet, and saw a lot of little bubbles – very little bubbles they were – rushing upward like a fan through the water outside. Steam! He felt the window, and it was hot. He turned on the minute glow-lamp that lit his own cavity, looked at the padded watch by the studs, and saw he had been travelling now for two minutes. It came into his head that the window would crack through the conflict of temperatures, for he knew the bottom water is very near freezing.

Then suddenly the floor of the sphere seemed to press against his feet, the rush of bubbles outside grew slower and slower, and the hissing diminished. The sphere rolled a little. The window had not cracked, nothing had given, and he knew that the dangers of sinking, at any rate, were over.

In another minute or so he would be on the floor of the abyss. He thought, he said, of Steevens and Weybridge and the rest of them five miles overhead, higher to him than the very highest clouds that ever floated over land are to us, steaming slowly and staring down and wondering what had happened to him.

He peered out of the window. There were no more bubbles now, and the hissing had stopped. Outside there was a heavy blackness – as black as black velvet – except where the electric light pierced the empty water and showed the colour of it – a yellow-green. Then three things like shapes of fire swam into sight, following each other through the water. Whether they were little and near or big and far off he could not tell.

Each was outlined in a bluish light almost as bright as the lights of a fishing smack, a light which seemed to be smoking greatly, and all along the sides of them were specks of this, like the lighter portholes of a ship. Their phosphorescence seemed to go out as they came into the radiance of his lamp, and he saw then that they were little fish of some strange sort, with huge heads, vast eyes, and dwindling bodies and tails. Their eyes were turned towards him, and he judged they were following him down. He supposed they were attracted by his glare.

Presently others of the same sort joined them. As he went on down, he noticed that the water became of a pallid colour, and that little specks twinkled in his ray like motes in a sunbeam. This was probably due to the clouds of ooze and mud that the impact of his leaden sinkers had disturbed.

By the time he was drawn down to the lead weights he was in a dense fog of white that his electric light failed altogether to pierce for more than a few yards, and many minutes elapsed before the hanging sheets of sediment subsided to any extent. Then, lit by his light and by the transient phosphorescence of a distant shoal of fishes, he was able to see under the huge blackness of the superincumbent water an undulating expanse of greyish-white ooze, broken here and there by tangled thickets of a growth of sea lilies, waving hungry tentacles in the air.

Farther away were the graceful, translucent outlines of a group of gigantic sponges. About this floor there were scattered a number of bristling flattish tufts of rich purple and black, which he decided must be some sort of sea-urchin, and small, large-eyed or blind things having a curious resemblance, some to woodlice, and other to lobsters, crawled sluggishly across the track of the light and vanished into the obscurity again, leaving furrowed trails behind them.

Then suddenly the hovering swarm of little fishes veered about and came towards him as a flight of starlings might do. They passed over him like a phosphorescent snow, and then he saw behind them some larger creature advancing towards the sphere.

At first he could see it only dimly, a faintly moving figure remotely suggestive of a walking man, and then it came into the spray of light that the lamp shot out. As the glare struck it, it shut its eyes, dazzled. He stared in rigid astonishment.

It was a strange vertebrated animal. Its dark purple head was dimly suggestive of a chameleon, but it had such a high forehead and such a braincase as no reptile ever displayed before; the vertical pitch of its face gave it a most extraordinary resemblance to a human being.

Two large and protruding eyes projected from sockets in chameleon fashion, and it had a broad reptilian mouth with horny lips beneath its little nostrils. In the position of the ears were two huge gill-covers, and out of these floated a branching tree of coralline filaments, almost like the tree-like gills that very young rays and sharks possess.

But the humanity of the face was not the most extraordinary thing about the creature. It was a biped; its almost globular body was poised on a tripod of two frog-like legs and a long thick tail, and its fore limbs, which grotesquely caricatured the human hand, much as a frog's do, carried a long shaft of bone, tipped with copper. The colour of the creature was variegated; its head, hands, and legs were purple; but its skin, which hung loosely upon it, even as clothes might do, was a phosphorescent grey. And it stood there blinded by the light.

At last this unknown creature of the abyss blinked its eyes open, and, shading them with its disengaged hand, opened its mouth and gave vent to a shouting noise, articulate almost as speech might be, that penetrated even the steel case and padded jacket of the sphere. How a shouting may be accomplished without lungs Elstead does not profess to explain. It then moved sideways out of the glare into the mystery of shadow that bordered it on either side, and Elstead felt rather than saw that it was coming towards him. Fancying the light had attracted it, he turned the switch that cut off the current. In another moment something soft dabbed upon the steel, and the globe swayed.

Then the shouting was repeated, and it seemed to him that a distant echo answered it. The dabbing recurred, and the whole globe swayed and ground against the spindle over which the wire was rolled. He stood in the blackness and peered out into the everlasting night of the abyss. And presently he saw, very faint and remote, other phosphorescent quasi-human forms hurrying towards him.

Hardly knowing what he did, he felt about in his swaying prison for the stud of the exterior electric light, and came by accident against his own small glow-lamp in its padded recess. The sphere twisted, and then threw him down; he heard shouts like shouts of surprise and when he rose to his feet he saw two pairs of stalked eyes peering into the lower window and reflecting his light.

In another moment hands were dabbing vigorously at his steel casing, and there was a sound, horrible enough in his position, of the metal protection of the clockwork being vigorously hammered. That, indeed, sent his heart into his mouth, for if these strange creatures succeeded in stopping that, his release would never occur. Scarcely had he thought as much when he felt the sphere sway violently, and the floor of it press hard against his feet. He turned off the small glow-lamp that lit the interior, and sent the ray of the large light in the separate compartment out into the water. The sea-floor and the man-like creatures had disappeared, and a couple of fish chasing each other dropped suddenly by the window.

He thought at once that these strange denizens of the deep sea had broken the rope, and that he had escaped. He drove up faster and faster, and then stopped with a jerk that sent him flying against the padded roof of his prison. For half a minute, perhaps, he was too astonished to think.

Then he felt that the sphere was spinning slowly, and rocking, and it seemed to him that it was also being drawn through the water. By crouching close to the window, he managed to make his weight effective and roll that part of the sphere downward, but he could see nothing save the pale ray of his light striking down ineffectively into the darkness. It occurred to him that he would see more if he turned the lamp off, and allowed his eyes to grow accustomed to the profound obscurity.

In this he was wise. After some minutes the velvety blackness became a translucent blackness, and then, far away, and as faint as the zodiacal light of an English summer evening, he saw shapes moving below. He judged these creatures had detached his cable and were towing him along the sea bottom.

And then he saw something faint and remote across the undulations of the submarine plain, a broad horizon of pale luminosity that extended this way and that way as far as the range of his little window permitted him to see. To this he was being towed, as a balloon might be towed by men out of the open country into a town. He approached it very slowly, and very slowly the dim irradiation was gathered together into more definite shapes.

It was nearly five o'clock before he came over this luminous area, and by that time he could make out an arrangement suggestive of streets and houses grouped about a vast roofless erection that was grotesquely suggestive of a ruined abbey. It was spread out like a map below him. The houses were all roofless enclosures of walls, and their substance being, as he afterwards saw, of phosphorescent bones, gave the place an appearance as if it were built of drowned moonshine.

Among the inner caves of the place waving trees of crinoid stretched their tentacles, and tall, slender, glassy sponges shot like shining minarets and lilies of filmy light out of the general glow of the city. In the open spaces of the place he could see a stirring movement as of crowds of people, but he was too many fathoms above them to distinguish the individuals in those crowds.

Then slowly they pulled him down, and as they did so, the details of the place crept slowly upon his apprehension. He saw that the courses of the cloudy buildings were marked out with beaded lines of round objects, and then he perceived that at several points below him, in broad open spaces, were forms like the encrusted shapes of ships.

Slowly and surely he was drawn down, and the forms below him became brighter, clearer, more distinct. He was being pulled down, he perceived, towards the large building in the centre of the town, and he could catch a glimpse ever and again of the multitudinous forms that were lugging at his cord. He was astonished to see that the rigging of one of the ships, which formed such a prominent feature of the place, was crowded with a host of gesticulating figures regarding him, and then the walls of the great building rose about him silently, and hid the city from his eyes.

And such walls they were, of water-logged wood, and twisted wire-rope, and iron spars, and copper, and the bones and skulls of dead men. The skulls ran in zigzag lines and spirals and fantastic curves over the buildings; and in and out of their eye-sockets, and over the whole surface of the place, lurked and played a multitude of silvery little fishes.

Suddenly his ears were filled with a low shouting and a noise like the violent blowing of horns, and this gave place to a fantastic chant. Down the sphere sank, past the huge pointed windows, through which he saw vaguely a great number of these strange ghostlike people regarding him, and at last he came to rest, as it seemed, on a kind of altar that stood in the centre of the place.

And now he was at such a level that he could see these strange people of the abyss plainly once more. To his astonishment, he perceived that they were prostrating themselves before him, all save one, dressed as it seemed in a robe of placoid scales, and crowned with a luminous diadem, who stood with his reptilian mouth opening and shutting, as though he led the chanting of the worshippers.

A curious impulse made Elstead turn on his small glow-lamp again, so that he became visible to these creatures of the abyss, albeit the glare made them disappear forthwith into night. At this sudden sight of him, the chanting gave place to a tumult of exultant shouts; and Elstead, being anxious to watch them, turned his light off again, and vanished from before their eyes. But for a time he was too blind to make out what they were doing, and when at last he could distinguish them, they were kneeling again. And thus they continued worshipping him, without rest or intermission, for a space of three hours.

Most circumstantial was Elstead's account of his astounding city and its people, these people of perpetual night, who have never seen sun or moon or stars, green vegetation, nor any living, air-breathing creatures, who know nothing of fire, nor any light but the phosphorescent light of living things.

Startling as is his story, it is yet more startling to find that scientific men, of such eminence as Adams and Jenkins, find nothing incredible in it. They tell me they see no reason why intelligent, water-breathing, vertebrated creatures inured to a low temperature and enormous pressure, and of such a heavy structure that neither alive nor dead would they float, might not live upon the bottom of the deep sea, and quite unsuspected by us, descendants like ourselves of the great Theriomorpha of the New Red Sandstone Age.

We should be known to them, however, as strange, meteoric creatures, wont to fall catastrophically dead out of the mysterious blackness of their watery sky. And not only we ourselves, but our ships, our metals, our appliances, would come raining down out of the night. Sometimes sinking things would smite down and crush them, as if it were the judgement of some unseen power above, and sometimes would come things of the utmost rarity or utility, or shapes of inspiring suggestion. One can understand, perhaps, something of their behaviour at the descent of a living man, if one thinks what a barbaric people might do, to whom an enhaloed, shining creature came suddenly out of the sky.

At one time or another Elstead probably told the officers of the *Ptarmigan* every detail of his strange twelve hours in the abyss. That he also intended to write them down is certain, but he never did, and so unhappily we have to piece together the discrepant fragments of his story from the reminiscences of Commander Simmons, Weybridge, Steevens, Lindley, and the others.

We see the thing darkly in fragmentary glimpses – the huge ghostly building, the bowing, chanting people, with their dark chameleonlike heads and faintly luminous clothing, and Elstead, with his light turned on again, vainly trying to convey to their minds that the cord by which the sphere was held was to be severed. Minute after minute slipped away, and Elstead, looking at his watch, was horrified to find that he had oxygen only for four hours more. But the chant in his honour kept on as remorselessly as if it was the marching song of his approaching death.

The manner of his release he does not understand, but to judge by the end of cord that hung from the sphere, it had been cut through by rubbing against the edge of the altar. Abruptly the sphere rolled over, and he swept up, out of their world, as an ethereal creature clothed in a vacuum would sweep through our own atmosphere back to its native ether again. He must have torn out of their sight as a hydrogen bubble hastens upward from our air. A strange ascension it must have seemed to them.

The sphere rushed up with even greater velocity than, when weighted with the lead sinkers, it had rushed down. It became exceedingly hot. It drove up with the windows uppermost, and he remembers the torrent of bubbles frothing against the glass. Every moment he expected this to fly. Then suddenly something like a huge wheel seemed to be released in his head, the padded compartment began spinning about him, and he fainted. His next recollection was of his cabin, and of the doctor's voice.

But that is the substance of the extraordinary story that Elstead related in fragments to the officers of the *Ptargiman*. He promised to write it all down at a later date. His mind was chiefly occupied with the improvement of his apparatus, which was effected at Rio.

It remains only to tell that on February 2, 1896, he made his second descent into the ocean abyss, with the improvements his first experience suggested. What happened we shall probably never know. He never returned. The *Ptarmigan* beat about over the point of his submersion, seeking him in vain for thirteen days. Then she returned to Rio, and the news was telegraphed to his friends. So the matter rests for the present. But it is hardly probable that no further attempt will be made to verify his strange story of these hitherto unsuspected cities of the deep sea.

The Machine Stops

E. M. FORSTER

The reputation of E. M. Forster *(*1879–1970*) rests largely on his work as a novelist –* Where Angels Fear to Tread *(*1905*),* The Longest Journey *(*1907*),* A Room with a View *(*1908*),* Howard's End *(*1910*) – but he has written a number of short stories too.*

In 1947*, when his short stories (all written before the First World War) were published in one volume for the first time, he introduced them by saying:*

> *'Fantasy today tends to retreat or to dig herself in or to become apocalyptic out of deference to the atom-bomb. She can be caught in the open here by those who care to catch her. She flits over the scenes of Italian and English holidays, or wings her way with even less justification towards the countries of the future.'*

The Machine Stops *is a science fantasy, admitted by Forster himself to be 'a reaction to one of the earlier heavens of* H. G. Wells*'. It is also 'a meditation', as the first paragraph of the story suggests.*

The story is a demonstration of the threat to human happiness posed by machines: 'We created the Machine, to do our will, but we cannot do our will now. It has robbed us of the sense of space and of the sense of touch, it has blurred every human relation and narrowed down love to a carnal act, it has paralysed our bodies and our wills, and now it compels us to worship it.' It is in reality 'anti-science fiction', in which the standards and claims of science are challenged by an ironic statement of its advantages.

As a science fantasy it has familiar, recognizable elements: a machine which man invented and which ultimately destroys him; it can provide communication, cold baths, food, beds (but in a standard size only), and it can recreate itself; it is horrifying in its totalitarian demands and the relentlessness with which it pursues them; if Man surrenders he must pay the price for the surrender of his will.

As a meditation the story relies heavily on irony: 'in certain directions human intercourse had advanced enormously'; 'dawn, mid-day, twilight, the zodiacal path, touched neither men's lives nor their hearts and science retreated into the ground'; 'how we have advanced, thanks to the Machine!' In spite of appearances science cannot satisfy all human needs – it can transmit expressions but not nuances of expression; 'human passion still blundered up and down in the Machine'; Vashti cries out to Kuno, 'But I can see you! What more do you want?' The ultimate condemnation of the Machine is, however, its destruction of further ideas: 'Let your ideas be second-hand, and if possible tenth-hand, for then they will be far removed from that disturbing element – direct observation' – the one thing on which science itself depends, ironically.

Science can destroy itself, as the Machine does, but the value of human dignity is vindicated even in the manner of its death.

PART I

THE AIR-SHIP

Imagine, if you can, a small room, hexagonal in shape, like the cell of a bee. It is lighted neither by window nor by lamp, yet it is filled with a soft radiance. There are no apertures for ventilation, yet the air is fresh. There are no musical instruments, and yet, at the moment that my meditation opens, this room is throbbing with melodious sounds. An armchair is in the centre, by its side a reading-desk – that is all the furniture. And in the arm-chair there sits a swaddled lump of flesh – a woman, about five feet high, with a face as white as a fungus. It is to her that the little room belongs.

An electric bell rang.

The woman touched a switch and the music was silent.

'I suppose I must see who it is,' she thought, and set her chair in motion. The chair, like the music, was worked by machinery, and it rolled her to the other side of the room, where the bell still rang importunately.

'Who is it?' she called. Her voice was irritable, for she had been interrupted often since the music began. She knew several thousand people; in certain directions human intercourse had advanced enormously.

But when she listened into the receiver, her white face wrinkled into smiles, and she said:

'Very well. Let us talk, I will isolate myself. I do not expect anything important will happen for the next five minutes – for I can give you fully five minutes, Kuno. Then I must deliver my lecture on "Music during the Australian Period".'

She touched the isolation knob, so that no one else could speak to her. Then she touched the lighting apparatus, and the little room was plunged into darkness.

'Be quick!' she called, her irritation returning. 'Be quick, Kuno; here I am in the dark wasting my time.'

But it was fully fifteen seconds before the round plate that she held in her hands began to glow. A faint blue light shot across it, darkening to purple, and presently she could see the image of her son, who lived on the other side of the earth, and he could see her.

'Kuno, how slow you are.'

He smiled gravely.

'I really believe you enjoy dawdling.'

'I have called you before, mother, but you were always busy or isolated. I have something particular to say.'

'What is it, dearest boy? Be quick. Why could you not send it by pneumatic post?'

'Because I prefer saying such a thing. I want—'

'Well?'

'I want you to come and see me.'

Vashti watched his face in the blue plate.

'But I can see you!' she exclaimed. 'What more do you want?'

'I want to see you not through the Machine,' said Kuno. 'I want to speak to you not through the wearisome Machine.'

'Oh, hush!' said his mother, vaguely shocked. 'You mustn't say anything against the Machine.'

'Why not?'

'One mustn't.'

'You talk as if a god had made the Machine,' cried the other. 'I believe that you pray to it when you are unhappy. Men made it, do not forget that. Great men, but men. The Machine is much, but it is not everything. I see something like you in this plate, but I do not see you. I hear something like you through this telephone, but I do not hear you. That is why I want you to come. Come and stop with me. Pay me a visit, so that we can meet face to face, and talk about the hopes that are in my mind.'

She replied that she could scarcely spare the time for a visit.

'The air-ship barely takes two days to fly between me and you.'

'I dislike air-ships.'

'Why?'

'I dislike seeing the horrible brown earth, and the sea, and the stars when it is dark. I get no ideas in an air-ship.'

'I do not get them anywhere else.'

'What kind of ideas can the air give you?'

He paused for an instant.

'Do you not know four big stars that form an oblong, and three stars close together in the middle of the oblong, and hanging from the stars, three other stars?'

'No, I do not. I dislike the stars. But did they give you an idea? How interesting; tell me.'

'I had an idea that they were like a man.'

'I do not understand.'

'The four big stars are the man's shoulders and his knees. The three stars in the middle are like the belts that men wore once, and the three stars hanging are like a sword.'

'A sword?'

'Men carried swords about with them, to kill animals and other men.'

'It does not strike me as a very good idea, but it is certainly original. When did it come to you first?'

'In the air-ship—' He broke off, and she fancied that he looked sad. She could not be sure, for the Machine did not transmit *nuances* of expression. It only gave a general idea of people – an idea that was good enough for all practical purposes, Vashti thought. The imponderable bloom, declared by a discredited philosophy to be the actual essence of intercourse, was rightly ignored by the Machine, just as the imponderable bloom of the grape was ignored by the manufacturers of artificial fruit. Something 'good enough' had long since been accepted by our race.

'The truth is,' he continued, 'that I want to see these stars again. They are curious stars. I want to see them not from the air-ship, but from the surface of the earth, as our ancestors did, thousands of years ago. I want to visit the surface of the earth.'

She was shocked again.

'Mother, you must come, if only to explain to me what is the harm of visiting the surface of the earth.'

'No harm,' she replied, controlling herself. 'But no advantage. The surface of the earth is only dust and mud, no life remains on it, and you would need a respirator, or the cold of the outer air would kill you. One dies immediately in the outer air.'

'I know; of course I shall take all precautions.'

'And besides—'

'Well?'

She considered, and chose her words with care. Her son had a queer temper, and she wished to dissuade him from the expedition.

'It is contrary to the spirit of the age,' she asserted.

'Do you mean by that, contrary to the Machine?'

'In a sense, but—'

His image in the blue plate faded.

'Kuno!'

He had isolated himself.

For a moment Vashti felt lonely.

Then she generated the light, and the sight of her room, flooded with radiance and studded with electric buttons, revived her. There were buttons and switches everywhere – buttons to call for food, for music, for clothing. There was the hot-bath button, by pressure of which a basin of (imitation) marble rose out of the floor, filled to the brim with a warm deodorized liquid. There was the cold-bath button. There was the button that produced literature. And there were of course the buttons by which she communicated with her friends. The room, though it contained nothing, was in touch with all that she cared for in the world.

Vashti's next move was to turn off the isolation switch, and all the accumulations of the last three minutes burst upon her. The room was filled with the noise of bells, and speaking-tubes. What was the new food like? Could she recommend it? Had she had any ideas lately? Might one tell her one's own ideas? Would she make an engagement to visit the public nurseries at an early date? – say this day month.

To most of these questions she replied with irritation – a growing quality in that accelerated age. She said that the new food was horrible. That she could not visit the public nurseries through press of engagements. That she had no ideas of her own but had just been told one – that four stars and three in the middle were like a man: she doubted there was much in it. Then she switched off her correspondents, for it was time to deliver her lecture on Australian music.

The clumsy system of public gatherings had been long since abandoned; neither Vashti nor her audience stirred from their rooms. Seated in her arm-chair she spoke, while they in their arm-chairs heard her, fairly well, and saw her, fairly well. She opened with a humorous account of music in the pre-Mongolian epoch, and went on to describe the great outburst of song that followed the Chinese conquest. Remote and primaeval as were the methods of I-San-So and the Brisbane school, she yet felt (she said) that study of them might repay the musician of to-day: they had freshness; they had, above all, ideas.

Her lecture, which lasted ten minutes, was well received, and at its conclusion she and many of her audience listened to a lecture on the sea; there were ideas to be got from the sea; the speaker had donned a respirator and visited it lately. Then she fed, talked to many friends, had a bath, talked again, and summoned her bed.

The bed was not to her liking. It was too large, and she had a feeling for a small bed. Complaint was useless, for beds were of the same dimension all over the world, and to have had an alternative size would have involved vast alterations in the Machine. Vashti isolated herself – it was necessary, for neither day nor night existed under the ground – and reviewed all that had happened since she had summoned the bed last. Ideas? Scarcely any. Events – was Kuno's invitation an event?

By her side, on the little reading-desk, was a survival from the ages of litter – one book. This was the Book of the Machine. In it were instructions against every possible contingency. If she was hot or cold or dyspeptic or at a loss for a word, she went to the book, and it told her which button to press. The Central Committee published it. In accordance with a growing habit, it was richly bound.

Sitting up in the bed, she took it reverently in her hands. She glanced round the glowing room as if someone might be watching her. Then, half ashamed, half joyful, she murmured 'O Machine! O Machine!' and raised the volume to her lips. Thrice she kissed it, thrice inclined her head, thrice she felt the delirium of acquiescence. Her ritual performed, she turned to page 1367, which gave the times of the departure of the air-ships from the island in the southern hemisphere, under whose soil she lived, to the island in the northern hemisphere, whereunder lived her son.

She thought, 'I have not the time.'

She made the room dark and slept; she awoke and made the room light; she ate and exchanged ideas with her friends, and listened to music and attended lectures; she made the room dark and slept. Above her, beneath her, and around her, the Machine hummed eternally; she did not notice the noise, for she had been born with it in her ears. The earth, carrying her, hummed as it sped through silence, turning her now to the invisible sun, now to the invisible stars. She awoke and made the room light.

'Kuno!'

'I will not talk to you,' he answered, 'until you come.'

'Have you been on the surface of the earth since we spoke last?'

His image faded.

Again she consulted the book. She became very nervous and lay back in her chair palpitating. Think of her as without teeth or hair. Presently she directed the chair to the wall, and pressed an unfamiliar button. The wall swung apart slowly. Through the opening she saw a tunnel that curved slightly, so that its goal was not visible. Should she go to see her son, here was the beginning of the journey.

Of course she knew all about the communication-system. There was nothing mysterious in it. She would summon a car and it would fly with her down the tunnel until it reached the lift that communicated with the air-ship station: the system had been in use for many, many years, long before the universal establishment of the Machine. And of course she had studied the civilization that had immediately preceded her own – the civilization that had mistaken the functions of the system, and had used it for bringing people to things, instead of for bringing things to people. Those funny old days, when men went for change of air instead of changing the air in their rooms! And yet – she was frightened of the tunnel: she had not seen it since her last child was born. It curved – but not quite as she remembered; it was brilliant – but not quite as brilliant as a lecturer had suggested. Vashti was seized with the terrors of direct experience. She shrank back into the room, and the wall closed up again.

'Kuno,' she said, 'I cannot come to see you. I am not well.'

Immediately an enormous apparatus fell on to her out of the ceiling, a thermometer was automatically inserted between her lips, a stethoscope was automatically laid upon her heart. She lay powerless. Cool pads soothed her forehead. Kuno had telegraphed to her doctor.

So the human passions still blundered up and down in the Machine. Vashti drank the medicine that the doctor projected into her mouth, and the machinery retired into the ceiling. The voice of Kuno was heard asking how she felt.

'Better.' Then with irritation: 'But why do you not come to me instead?'

'Because I cannot leave this place.'

'Why?'

'Because, any moment, something tremendous may happen.'

'Have you been on the surface of the earth yet?'

'Not yet.'

'Then what is it?'

'I will not tell you through the Machine.'

She resumed her life.

But she thought of Kuno as a baby, his birth, his removal to the public nurseries, her one visit to him there, his visits to her – visits which stopped when the Machine had assigned him a room on the other side of the earth. 'Parents, duties of,' said the book of the Machine, 'cease at the moment of birth. P.422327483.' True, but there was something special about Kuno – indeed there had been something special about all her children – and after all, she must brave the journey if he desired it. And 'something tremendous might happen'. What did that mean? The nonsense of a youthful man, no doubt, but she must go. Again she pressed the unfamiliar button, again the wall swung back, and she saw the tunnel that curved out of sight. Clasping the Book, she rose, tottered on to the platform, and summoned the car. Her room closed behind her: the journey to the northern hemisphere had begun.

Of course it was perfectly easy. The car approached and in it she found arm-chairs exactly like her own. When she signalled, it stopped, and she tottered into the lift. One other passenger was in the lift, the first fellow creature she had seen face to face for months. Few travelled in these days, for, thanks to the advance of science, the earth was exactly alike all over. Rapid intercourse, from which the previous civilization had hoped so much, had ended by defeating itself. What was the good of going to Pekin when it was just like Shrewsbury? Why return to Shrewsbury when it would be just like Pekin? Men seldom moved their bodies; all unrest was concentrated in the soul.

The air-ship service was a relic from the former age. It was kept up, because it was easier to keep it up than to stop it or to diminish it, but it now far exceeded the wants of the population. Vessel after vessel would rise from the vomitories of Rye or of Christchurch (I use the antique names), would sail into the crowded sky, and would draw up at the wharves of the south – empty. So nicely adjusted was the system, so independent of meteorology, that the sky, whether calm or cloudy, resembled a vast kaleidoscope whereon the same patterns periodically recurred. The ship on which Vashti sailed started now at sunset, now at dawn. But always, as it passed above Rheims, it would neighbour the ship that served between Helsingfors and the Brazils, and, every third time it surmounted the Alps, the fleet of Palermo would cross its track behind. Night and day, wind and storm, tide and earthquake, impeded man no longer. He had harnessed Leviathan. All the old literature, with its praise of Nature, and its fear of Nature, rang false as the prattle of a child.

Yet as Vashti saw the vast flank of the ship, stained with exposure to the outer air, her horror of direct experience returned. It was not quite like the air-ship in the cinematophote. For one thing it smelt – not strongly or unpleasantly, but it did smell, and with her eyes shut she should have known that a new thing was close to her. Then she had to walk to it from the lift, had to submit to glances from the other passengers. The man in front dropped his Book – no great matter, but it disquieted them all. In the rooms, if the Book was dropped, the floor raised it mechanically, but the gangway to the air-ship was not so prepared, and the sacred volume lay motionless. They stopped – the thing was unforeseen – and the man, instead of picking up his property, felt the muscles of his arm to see how they had failed him. Then some one actually said with direct utterance: 'We shall be late' – and they trooped on board, Vashti treading on the pages as she did so.

Inside, her anxiety increased. The arrangements were old-fashioned and rough. There was even a female attendant, to whom she would have to announce her wants during the voyage. Of course a revolving platform ran the length of the boat, but she was expected to walk from it to her cabin. Some cabins were better than others, and she did not get the best. She thought the attendant had been unfair, and spasms of rage shook her. The glass valves had closed, she could not go back. She saw, at the end of the vestibule, the lift in which she had ascended going quietly up and down, empty. Beneath those corridors of shining tiles were rooms, tier below tier, reaching far into the earth, and in each room there sat a human being, eating, or sleeping, or producing ideas. And buried deep in the hive was her own room. Vashti was afraid.

'O Machine! O Machine!' she murmured, and caressed her Book, and was comforted.

Then the sides of the vestibule seemed to melt together, as do the passages that we see in dreams, the lift vanished, the Book that had been dropped slid to the left and vanished, polished tiles rushed by like a stream of water, there was a slight jar, and the air-ship, issuing from its tunnel, soared above the waters of a tropical ocean.

It was night. For a moment she saw the coast of Sumatra edged by the phosphorescence of waves, and crowned by lighthouses, still sending forth their disregarded beams. These also vanished, and only the stars distracted her. They were not motionless, but swayed to and fro above her head, thronging out of one sky-light into another, as if the universe and not the air-ship was careening. And, as often happens on clear nights, they seemed now to be in perspective, now on a plane; now piled tier beyond tier into the infinite heavens, now concealing infinity, a roof limiting for ever the visions of men. In either case they seemed intolerable. 'Are we to travel in the dark?' called the passengers angrily, and the attendant, who had been careless, generated the light, and pulled down the blinds of pliable metal. When the air-ships had been built, the desire to look direct at things still lingered in the world. Hence the extraordinary number of skylights and windows, and the proportionate discomfort to those who were civilized and refined. Even in Vashti's cabin one star peeped through a flaw in the blind, and after a few hours' uneasy slumber, she was disturbed by an unfamiliar glow, which was the dawn.

Quick as the ship had sped westwards, the earth had rolled eastwards quicker still, and had dragged back Vashti and her companions towards the sun. Science could prolong the night, but only for a little, and those high hopes of neutralizing the earth's diurnal revolution had passed, together with hopes that were possibly higher. To 'keep pace with the sun,' or even to outstrip it, had been the aim of the civilization preceding this. Racing aeroplanes had been built for the purpose, capable of enormous speed, and steered by the greatest intellects of the epoch. Round the globe they went, round and round, westward, westward, round and round, amidst humanity's applause. In vain. The globe went eastward quicker still, horrible accidents occurred, and the Committee of the Machine, at the time rising into prominence, declared the pursuit illegal, unmechanical, and punishable by Homelessness.

Of Homelessness more will be said later.

Doubtless the Committee was right. Yet the attempt to 'defeat the sun' aroused the last common interest that our race experienced about the heavenly bodies, or indeed about anything. It was the last time that men were compacted by thinking of a power outside the world. The sun had conquered, yet it was the end of his spiritual dominion. Dawn, mid-day, twilight, the zodiacal path, touched neither men's lives nor their hearts, and science retreated into the ground, to concentrate herself upon problems that she was certain of solving.

So when Vashti found her cabin invaded by a rosy finger of light, she was annoyed, and tried to adjust the blind. But the blind flew up altogether, and she saw through the skylight small pink clouds, swaying against a background of blue, and as the sun crept higher, its radiance entered direct, brimming down the wall, like a golden sea. It rose and fell with the air-ship's motion, just as waves rise and fall, but it advanced steadily, as a tide advances. Unless she was careful, it would strike her face. A spasm of horror shook her and she rang for the attendant. The attendant too was horrified, but she could do nothing; it was not her place to mend the blind. She could only suggest that the lady should change her cabin, which she accordingly prepared to do.

People were almost exactly alike all over the world, but the attendant of the air-ship, perhaps owing to her exceptional duties, had grown a little out of the common. She had often to address passengers with direct speech, and this had given her a certain roughness and originality of manner. When Vashti swerved away from the sunbeams with a cry, she behaved barbarically – she put out her hand to steady her.

'How dare you!' exclaimed the passenger. 'You forget yourself!'

The woman was confused, and apologized for not having let her fall. People never touched one another. The custom had become obsolete, owing to the Machine.

'Where are we now?' asked Vashti haughtily.

'We are over Asia,' said the attendant, anxious to be polite.

'Asia?'

'You must excuse my common way of speaking. I have got into the habit of calling places over which I pass by their unmechanical names.'

'Oh, I remember Asia. The Mongols came from it.'

'Beneath us, in the open air, stood a city that was once called Simla.'

'Have you never heard of the Mongols and of the Brisbane school?'

'No.'

'Brisbane also stood in the open air.'

'Those mountains to the right – let me show you them.' She pushed back a metal blind. The main chain of the Himalayas was revealed. 'They were once called the Roof of the World, those mountains.'

'What a foolish name!'

'You must remember that, before the dawn of civilization, they seemed to be an impenetrable wall that touched the stars. It was supposed that no one but the gods could exist above their summits. How we have advanced, thanks to the Machine!'

'How we have advanced, thanks to the Machine!' said Vashti.

'How we have advanced, thanks to the Machine!' echoed the passenger who had dropped his Book the night before, and who was standing in the passage.

'And that white stuff in the cracks? – what is it?'

'I have forgotten its name.'

'Cover the window, please. These mountains give me no ideas.'

The northern aspect of the Himalayas was in deep shadow: on the Indian slope the sun had just prevailed. The forests had been destroyed during the literature epoch for the purpose of making newspaper-pulp, but the snows were awakening to their morning glory, and clouds still hung on the breasts of Kinchinjunga. In the plain were seen the ruins of cities, with diminished rivers creeping by their walls, and by the sides of these were sometimes the signs of vomitories, marking the cities of to-day. Over the whole prospect air-ships rushed, crossing and intercrossing with incredible *aplomb*, and rising nonchalantly when they desired to escape the perturbations of the lower atmosphere and to traverse the Roof of the World.

'We have indeed advanced, thanks to the Machine,' repeated the attendant, and hid the Himalayas behind a metal blind.

The day dragged wearily forward. The passengers sat each in his cabin, avoiding one another with an almost physical repulsion and longing to be once more under the surface of the earth. There were eight or ten of them, mostly young males, sent out from the public nurseries to inhabit the rooms of those who had died in various parts of the earth. The man who had dropped his Book was on the homeward journey. He had been sent to Sumatra for the purpose of propagating the race. Vashti alone was travelling by her private will.

At midday she took a second glance at the earth. The air-ship was crossing another range of mountains, but she could see little, owing to clouds. Masses of black rock hovered below her, and merged indistinctly into grey. Their shapes were fantastic; one of them resembled a prostrate man.

'No ideas here,' murmured Vashti, and hid the Caucasus behind a metal blind.

In the evening she looked again. They were crossing a golden sea, in which lay many small islands and one peninsula.

She repeated, 'No ideas here,' and hid Greece behind a metal blind.

PART II

THE MENDING APPARATUS

By a vestibule, by a lift, by a tubular railway, by a platform, by a sliding door – by reversing all the steps of her departure did Vashti arrive at her son's room, which exactly resembled her own. She might well declare that the visit was superfluous. The buttons, the knobs, the reading-desk with the Book, the temperature, the atmosphere, the illumination – all were exactly the same. And if Kuno himself, flesh of her flesh, stood close beside her at last, what profit was there in that? She was too well-bred to shake him by the hand.

Averting her eyes, she spoke as follows:

'Here I am. I have had the most terrible journey and greatly retarded the development of my soul. It is not worth it, Kuno, it is not worth it. My time is too precious. The sunlight almost touched me, and I have met with the rudest people. I can only stop a few minutes. Say what you want to say, and then I must return.'

'I have been threatened with Homelessness,' said Kuno.

She looked at him now.

'I have been threatened with Homelessness, and I could not tell you such a thing through the Machine.'

Homelessness means death. The victim is exposed to the air, which kills him.

'I have been outside since I spoke to you last. The tremendous thing has happened, and they have discovered me.'

'But why shouldn't you go outside?' she exclaimed. 'It is perfectly legal, perfectly mechanical, to visit the surface of the earth. I have lately been to a lecture on the sea; there is no objection to that; one simply summons a respirator and gets an Egression-permit. It is not the kind of thing that spiritually-minded people do, and I begged you not to do it, but there is no legal objection to it.'

'I did not get an Egression-permit.'

'Then how did you get out?'

'I found out a way of my own.'

The phrase conveyed no meaning to her, and he had to repeat it.

'A way of your own?' she whispered. 'But that would be wrong.'

'Why?'

The question shocked her beyond measure.

'You are beginning to worship the Machine,' he said coldly. 'You think it irreligious of me to have found out a way of my own. It was just what the Committee thought, when they threatened me with Homelessness.'

At this she grew angry. 'I worship nothing!' she cried. 'I am most advanced. I don't think you irreligious, for there is no such thing as religion left. All the fear and the superstition that existed once have been destroyed by the Machine. I only meant that to find out a way of your own was— Besides, there is no new way out.'

'So it is always supposed.'

'Except through the vomitories, for which one must have an Egression-permit, it is impossible to get out. The Book says so.'

'Well, the Book's wrong, for I have been out on my feet.'

For Kuno was possessed of a certain physical strength.

By these days it was a demerit to be muscular. Each infant was examined at birth, and all who promised undue strength were destroyed. Humanitarians may protest, but it would have been no true kindness to let an athlete live; he would never have been happy in that state of life to which the Machine had called him; he would have yearned for trees to climb, rivers to bathe in, meadows and hills against which he might measure his body. Man must be adapted to his surroundings, must he not? In the dawn of the world our weakly must be exposed on Mount Taygetus; in its twilight our strong will suffer euthanasia, that the Machine may progress, that the Machine may progress, that the Machine may progress eternally.

'You know that we have lost the sense of space. We say "space is annihilated", but we have annihilated not space, but the sense thereof. We have lost a part of ourselves. I determined to recover it, and I began by walking up and down the platform of the railway outside my room. Up and down, until I was tired, and so did recapture the meaning of "Near" and "Far". "Near" is a place to which I can get quickly *on my feet,* not a place to which the train or the air-ship will take me quickly. "Far" is a place to which I cannot get quickly on my feet; the vomitory is "far", though I could be there in thirty-eight seconds by summoning the train. Man is the measure. That was my first lesson. Man's feet are the measure for distance, his hands are the measure for ownership, his body is the measure for all that is lovable and desirable and strong. Then I went further: it was then that I called to you for the first time, and you would not come.

'This city, as you know, is built deep beneath the surface of the earth, with only the vomitories protruding. Having paced the platform outside my own room, I took the lift to the next platform and paced that also, and so with each in turn, until I came to the topmost, above which begins the earth. All the platforms were exactly alike, and all that I gained by visiting them was to develop my sense of space and my muscles. I think I should have been content with this – it is not a little thing, – but as I walked and brooded, it occurred to me that our cities had been built in the days when men still breathed the outer air, and that there had been ventilation shafts for the workmen. I could think of nothing but these ventilation shafts. Had they been destroyed by all the food-tubes and medicine-tubes and music-tubes that the Machine has evolved lately? Or did traces of them remain? One thing was certain. If I came upon them anywhere, it would be in the railway-tunnels of the topmost story. Everywhere else, all space was accounted for.

'I am telling my story quickly, but don't think that I was not a coward or that your answers never depressed me. It is not the proper thing, it is not mechanical, it is not decent to walk along a railway-tunnel. I did not fear that I might tread upon a live rail and be killed. I feared something far more intangible—doing what was not contemplated by the Machine. Then I said to myself, "Man is the measure," and I went, and after many visits I found an opening.

'The tunnels, of course, were lighted. Everything is light, artificial light; darkness is the exception. So when I saw a black gap in the tiles, I knew that it was an exception, and rejoiced. I put in my arm – I could put in no more at first – and waved it round and round in ecstasy. I loosened another tile, and put in my head, and shouted into the darkness: "I am coming, I shall do it yet," and my voice reverberated down endless passages. I seemed to hear the spirits of those dead workmen who had returned each evening to the starlight and to their wives, and all the generations who had lived in the open air called back to me, "You will do it yet, you are coming." '

He paused, and, absurd as he was, his last words moved her. For Kuno had lately asked to be a father, and his request had been refused by the Committee. His was not a type that the Machine desired to hand on.

'Then a train passed. It brushed by me, but I thrust my head and arms into the hole. I had done enough for one day, so I crawled back to the platform, went down in the lift, and summoned my bed. Ah what dreams! And again I called you, and again you refused.'

She shook her head and said:

'Don't. Don't talk of these terrible things. You make me miserable. You are throwing civilization away.'

'But I had got back the sense of space and a man cannot rest then. I determined to get in at the hole and climb the shaft. And so I exercised my arms. Day after day I went through ridiculous movements, until my flesh ached, and I could hang by my hands and hold the pillow of my bed outstretched for many minutes. Then I summoned a respirator, and started.

'It was easy at first. The mortar had somehow rotted, and I soon pushed some more tiles in, and clambered after them into the darkness, and the spirits of the dead comforted me. I don't know what I mean by that. I just say what I felt. I felt, for the first time, that a protest had been lodged against corruption, and that even as the dead were comforting the unborn. I felt that humanity existed, and that it existed without clothes. How can I possibly explain this? It was naked, humanity seemed naked, and all these tubes and buttons and machineries neither came into the world with us, nor will they follow us out, nor do they matter supremely while we are here. Had I been strong, I would have torn off every garment I had, and gone out into the outer unswaddled. But this is not for me, nor perhaps for my generation. I climbed with my respirator and my hygienic clothes and my dietetic tabloids! Better thus than not at all.

'There was a ladder, made of some primaeval metal. The light from the railway fell upon its lowest rungs, and I saw that it led straight upwards out of the rubble at the bottom of the shaft. Perhaps our ancestors ran up and down it a dozen times daily, in their building. As I climbed, the rough edges cut through my gloves so that my hands bled. The light helped me for a little, and then came darkness and, worse still, silence which pierced my ears like a sword. The

Machine hums! Did you know that? Its hum penetrates our blood, and may even guide our thoughts. Who knows! I was getting beyond its power. Then I thought: "This silence means that I am doing wrong." But I heard voices in the silence, and again they strengthened me.' He laughed. 'I had need of them. The next moment I cracked my head against something.'

She sighed.

'I had reached one of those pneumatic stoppers that defend us from the outer air. You may have noticed them on the air-ship. Pitch dark, my feet on the rungs of an invisible ladder, my hands cut; I cannot explain how I lived through this part, but the voices still comforted me, and I felt for fastenings. The stopper, I suppose was about eight feet across. I passed my hand over it as far as I could reach. It was perfectly smooth. I felt it almost to the centre. Not quite to the centre, for my arm was too short. Then the voice said: "Jump. It is worth it. There may be a handle in the centre, and you may catch hold of it and so come to us your own way. And if there is no handle, so that you may fall and are dashed to pieces – it is still worth it: you will still come to us your own way." So I jumped. There was a handle, and—'

He paused. Tears gathered in his mother's eyes. She knew that he was fated. If he did not die to-day he would die to-morrow. There was not room for such a person in the world. And with her pity disgust mingled. She was ashamed at having borne such a son, she who had always been so respectable and so full of ideas. Was he really the little boy to whom she had taught the use of his stops and buttons, and to whom she had given his first lessons in the Book? The very hair that disfigured his lip showed that he was reverting to some savage type. On atavism the Machine can have no mercy.

'There was a handle, and I did catch it. I hung tranced over the darkness and heard the hum of these workings as the last whisper in a dying dream. All the things I had cared about and all the people I had spoken to through tubes appeared infinitely little. Meanwhile the handle revolved. My weight had set something in motion and I span slowly, and then—

'I cannot describe it. I was lying with my face to the sunshine. Blood poured from my nose and ears and I heard a tremendous roaring. The stopper, with me clinging to it, had simply been blown out of the earth, and the air that we make down here was escaping through the vent into the air above. It burst up like a fountain. I crawled back to it – for the upper air hurts – and, as it were, I took great sips from the edge. My respirator had flown goodness knows where, my clothes were torn. I just lay with my lips close to the hole, and I sipped until the bleeding stopped. You can imagine nothing so curious. This hollow in the grass – I will speak of it in a minute – the sun shining into it, not brilliantly but through marbled clouds, – the peace, the nonchalance, the sense of space, and, brushing my cheek, the roaring fountain of our artificial air! Soon I spied my respirator, bobbing up and down in the current high above my head, and higher still were many air-ships. But no one ever looks out of air-ships and in any case they could not have picked me up. There I was, stranded. The sun shone a little way down the shaft, and revealed the topmost rung of the ladder, but it was hopeless trying to reach it. I should either have been tossed up again by the escape, or else have fallen in, and died. I could only lie on the grass, sipping and sipping, and from time to time glancing around me.

'I knew that I was in Wessex, for I had taken care to go to a lecture on the subject before starting. Wessex lies above the room in which we are talking now. It was once an important state. Its kings held all the southern coast from the Andredswald to Cornwall, while the Wansdyke protected them on the north, running over the high ground. The lecturer was only concerned with the rise of Wessex, so I do not know how long it remained an international power, nor would the knowledge have assisted me. To tell the truth I could do nothing but laugh, during this part. There was I, with a pneumatic stopper by my side and a respirator bobbing over my head, imprisoned, all three of us, in a grass-grown hollow that was edged with fern.'

Then he grew grave again.

'Lucky for me that it was a hollow. For the air began to fall back into it and to fill it as water fills a bowl. I could crawl about. Presently I stood. I breathed a mixture, in which the air that hurts predominated whenever I tried to climb the sides. This was not so bad. I had not lost my tabloids and remained ridiculously cheerful, and as for the Machine, I forgot about it altogether. My one aim now was to get to the top, where the ferns were, and to view whatever objects lay beyond.

'I rushed the slope. The new air was still too bitter for me and I came rolling back, after a momentary vision of something grey. The sun grew feeble, and I remembered that he was in Scorpio – I had been to a lecture on that too. If the sun is in Scorpio, and you are in Wessex, it means that you must be as quick as you can, or it will get too dark. (This is the first bit of useful information I have ever got from a lecture, and I expect it will be the last.) It made me try frantically to breathe the new air, and to advance as far as I dared out of my pond. The hollow filled so slowly. At times I thought that the fountain played with less vigour. My respirator seemed to dance nearer the earth; the roar was decreasing.'

He broke off.

'I don't think this is interesting you. The rest will interest you even less. There are no ideas in it, and I wish that I had not troubled you to come. We are too different, mother.'

She told him to continue.

'It was evening before I climbed the bank. The sun had very nearly slipped out of the sky by this time, and I could not get a good view. You, who have just crossed the Roof of the World, will not want to hear an account of the little hills that I saw – low colourless hills. But to me they were living and the turf that covered them was a skin, under which their muscles rippled, and I felt that those hills had called with incalculable force to men in the past, and that men had loved them. Now they sleep – perhaps for ever. They commune with humanity in dreams. Happy the man, happy the woman, who awakes in the hills of Wessex. For though they sleep they will never die.'

His voice rose passionately.

'Cannot you see, cannot all you lecturers see, that it is we that are dying, and that down here the only thing that really lives is the Machine? We created the Machine, to do our will, but we cannot make it do our will now. It has robbed us of the sense of space and of the sense of touch, it has blurred every human relation and narrowed down love to a carnal act, it has paralysed our bodies and our wills, and now it compels us to worship it. The Machine develops – but not on our lines. The Machine proceeds – but not to our goal. We only exist as the blood corpuscles that course through its arteries, and if it could work without us, it would let us die. Oh, I have no remedy – or, at least, only one—to tell men again and again that I have seen the hills of Wessex as Ælfrid saw them when he overthrew the Danes.

'So the sun set. I forgot to mention that a belt of mist lay between my hill and other hills, and that it was the colour of pearl.'

He broke off for the second time.

'Go on,' said his mother wearily.

He shook his head.

'Go on. Nothing that you can say can distress me now. I am hardened.'

'I had meant to tell you the rest, but I cannot: I know that I cannot: good-bye.'

Vashti stood irresolute. All her nerves were tingling with his blasphemies. But she was also inquisitive.

'This is unfair,' she complained. 'You have called me across the world to hear your story, and hear it I will. Tell me – as briefly as possible, for this is a disastrous waste of time – tell me how you returned to civilization.'

'Oh – that!' he said, starting. 'You would like to hear about civilization. Certainly. Had I got to where my respirator fell down?'

'No – but I understand everything now. You put on your respirator, and managed to walk along the surface of the earth to a vomitory, and there your conduct was reported to the Central Committee.'

'By no means.'

He passed his hand over his forehead, as if dispelling some strong impression. Then, resuming his narrative, he warmed to it again.

'My respirator fell about sunset. I had mentioned that the fountain seemed feebler, had I not?'

'Yes.'

'About sunset, it let the respirator fall. As I said, I had entirely forgotten about the Machine, and I paid no great attention at the time, being occupied with other things. I had my pool of air, into which I could dip when the outer keenness became intolerable, and which would possibly remain for days, provided that no wind sprang up to disperse it. Not until it was too late did I realize what the stoppage of the escape implied. You see – the gap in the tunnel had been mended; the Mending Apparatus; the Mending Apparatus, was after me.

'One other warning I had, but I neglected it. The sky at night was clearer than it had been in the day, and the moon, which was about half the sky behind the sun, shone into the dell at moments quite brightly. I was in my usual place – on the boundary between two atmospheres – when I thought I saw something dark move across the bottom of the dell, and vanish into the shaft. In my folly, I ran down. I bent over and listened, and I thought I heard a faint scraping noise in the depths.

'At this – but it was too late – I took alarm. I determined to put on my respirator and to walk right out of the dell. But my respirator had gone. I knew exactly where it had fallen – between the stopper and the aperture – and I could even feel the mark that it had made in the turf. It had gone, and I realized that something evil was at work, and I had better escape to the other air, and, if I must die, die running towards the cloud that had been the colour of a pearl. I never started. Out of the shaft – it is too horrible. A worm, a long white worm, had crawled out of the shaft and was gliding over the moonlit grass.

'I screamed. I did everything that I should not have done, I stamped upon the creature instead of flying from it, and it at once curled round the ankle. Then we fought. The worm let me run all over the dell, but edged up my leg as I ran. "Help!" I cried. (That part is too awful. It belongs to the part that you will never know.) "Help!" I cried. (Why cannot we suffer in silence?) "Help!" I cried. Then my feet were wound together, I fell, I was dragged away from the dear ferns and the living hills, and past the great metal stopper (I can tell you this part), and I thought it might save me again if I caught hold of the handle. It also was enwrapped, it also. Oh, the whole dell was full of the things. They were searching it in all directions, they were denuding it, and the white snouts of others peeped out of the hole, ready if needed. Everything that could be moved they brought – brushwood, bundles of fern, everything, and down we all went intertwined into hell. The last things that I saw, ere the stopper closed after us, were certain stars, and I felt that a man of my sort lived in the sky. For I did fight, I fought till the very end, and it was only my head hitting against the ladder that quieted me. I woke up in this room. The worms had vanished. I was surrounded by artificial air, artificial light, artificial peace, and my friends were calling to me down speaking-tubes to know whether I had come across any new ideas lately.'

Here his story ended. Discussion of it was impossible, and Vashti turned to go.

'It will end in Homelessness,' she said quietly.

'I wish it would,' retorted Kuno.

'The Machine has been most merciful.'

'I prefer the mercy of God.'

'By that superstitious phrase, do you mean that you could live in the outer air?'

'Yes.'

'Have you ever seen, round the vomitories, the bones of those who were extruded after the Great Rebellion?'

'Yes.'

'They were left where they perished for our edification. A few crawled away, but they perished, too – who can doubt it? And so with the Homeless of our own day. The surface of the earth supports life no longer.'

'Indeed.'

'Ferns and a little grass may survive, but all higher forms have perished. Has any air-ship detected them?'

'No.'

'Has any lecturer dealt with them?'

'No.'

'Then why this obstinacy?'

'Because I have seen them!' he exploded.

'Seen *what*?'

'Because I have seen her in the twilight – because she came to my help when I called – because she, too, was entangled by the worms, and, luckier than I, was killed by one of them piercing her throat.'

He was mad. Vashti departed, nor, in the troubles that followed, did she ever see his face again.

PART III

THE HOMELESS

During the years that followed Kuno's escapade, two important developments took place in the Machine. On the surface they were revolutionary, but in either case men's minds had been prepared beforehand, and they did but express tendencies that were latent already.

The first of these was the abolition of respirators.

Advanced thinkers, like Vashti, had always held it foolish to visit the surface of the earth. Air-ships might be necessary, but what was the good of going out for mere curiosity and crawling along for a mile or two in a terrestrial motor? The habit was vulgar and perhaps faintly improper: it was unproductive of ideas, and had no connection with the habits that really mattered. So respirators were abolished, and with them, of course, the terrestrial motors, and except for a few lecturers, who complained that they were debarred access to their subject-matter, the development was accepted quietly. Those who still wanted to know what the earth was like had after all only to listen to some gramophone, or to look into some cinematophote. And even the lecturers acquiesced when they found that a lecture on the sea was none the less stimulationg when compiled out of other lectures that had already been delivered on the same subject. 'Beware of first-hand ideas!' exclaimed one of the most advanced of them. 'First-hand ideas do not really exist. They are but the physical impressions produced by love and fear, and on this gross foundation who could erect a philosophy? Let your ideas be second hand, and if possible tenth-hand, for then they will be far removed from that disturbing element – direct observation. Do not learn anything about this subject of mine – the French Revolution. Learn instead what I think that Enicharmon thought Urizen thought Gutch thought Ho-Yung thought Chi-Bo-Sing thought Lafcadio Hearn thought Carlyle thought Mirabeau said about the French Revolution. Through the medium of these ten great minds, the blood that was shed at Paris and the windows that were broken at Versailles will be clarified to an idea which you may employ most profitably in your daily lives. But be sure that the intermediates are many and varied, for in history one authority exists to counteract another. Urizen must counteract the scepticism of Ho-Yung and Enicharmon, I must myself counteract the impetuosity of Gutch. You who listen to me are in a better position to judge about the French Revolution than I am. Your descendants will be even in a better position than you, for they will learn what you think I think, and yet another intermediate will be added to the chain. And in time – his voice rose – 'there will come a generation that has got beyond facts, beyond impressions, a generation absolutely colourless, a generation

> *. . . seraphically free*
> *From taint of personality,*

which will see the French Revolution not as it happened, nor as they would like it to have happened, but as it would have happened, had it taken place in the days of the Machine.'

Tremendous applause greeted this lecture, which did but voice a feeling already latent in the minds of men – a feeling that terrestrial facts must be ignored, and that the abolition of respirators was a positive gain. It was even suggested that air-ships should be abolished too. This was not done, because air-ships had somehow worked themselves into the Machine's system. But year by year they were used less, and mentioned less by thoughtful men.

The second great development was the re-establishment of religion.

This, too, had been voiced in the celebrated lecture. No one could mistake the reverent tone in which the peroration had concluded, and it awakened a responsive echo in the heart of each. Those who had long worshipped silently, now began to talk. They described the strange feeling of peace that came over them when they handled the Book of the Machine, the pleasure that it was to repeat certain numerals out of it, however little meaning those numerals conveyed to the outward ear, the ecstasy of touching a button, however unimportant, or of ringing an electric bell, however superfluously.

'The Machine,' they exclaimed, 'feeds us and clothes us and houses us; through it we speak to one another, through it we see one another, in it we have our being. The Machine is the friend of ideas and the enemy of superstition: the Machine is omnipotent, eternal; blessed is the Machine.' And before long this allocution was printed on the first page of the Book, and in subsequent editions the ritual swelled into a complicated system of praise and prayer. The word 'religion' was sedulously avoided, and in theory the Machine was still the creation and the implement of man. But in practice all, save a few retrogrades, worshipped it as divine. Nor was it worshipped in unity. One believer would be chiefly impressed by the blue optic plates, through which he saw other believers; another by the mending apparatus, which sinful Kuno had compared to worms; another by the lifts, another by the Book. And each would pray to this or to that, and ask it to intercede for him with the Machine as a whole. Persecution – that also was present. It did not break out, for reasons that will be set forward shortly. But it was latent, and all who did not accept the minimum known as 'undenominational Mechanism' lived in danger of Homelessness, which means death, as we know.

To attribute these two great developments to the Central Committee, is to take a very narrow view of civilization. The Central Committee announced the developments, it is true, but they were no more the cause of them than were the kings of the imperialistic period the cause of war. Rather did they yield to some invincible pressure, which came no one knew whither, and which, when gratified, was succeeded by some new pressure equally invincible. To such a state of affairs it is convenient to give the name of progress. No one confessed the Machine was out of hand. Year by year it was served with increased efficiency and decreased intelligence. The better a man knew his own duties upon it, the less he understood the duties of his neighbour, and in all the world there was not one who understood the monster as a whole. Those master brains had perished. They had left full directions, it is true, and their successors had each of them mastered a portion of those directions. But Humanity, in its desire for comfort, had over-reached itself. It had exploited the riches of nature too far. Quietly and complacently, it was sinking into decadence, and progress had come to mean the progress of the Machine.

As for Vashti, her life went peacefully forward until the final disaster. She made her room dark and slept; she awoke and made the room light. She lectured and attended lectures. She exchanged ideas with her innumerable friends and believed she was growing more spiritual. At times a friend was granted Euthanasia, and left his or her room for the homelessness that is beyond all human conception. Vashti did not much mind. After an unsuccessful lecture, she would sometimes ask for Euthanasia herself. But the death-rate was not permitted to exceed the birth-rate, and the Machine had hitherto refused it to her.

The troubles began quietly, long before she was conscious of them.

One day she was astonished at receiving a message from her son. They never communicated, having nothing in common, and she had only heard indirectly that he was still alive, and had been transferred from the northern hemisphere, where he had behaved so mischievously, to the southern – indeed, to a room not far from her own.

'Does he want me to visit him?' she thought. 'Never again, never. And I have not the time.'

No, it was madness of another kind.

He refused to visualize his face upon the blue plate, and speaking out of the darkness with solemnity said:

'The Machine stops.'

'What do you say?'

'The Machine is stopping, I know it. I know the signs.'

She burst into a peal of laughter. He heard her and was angry, and they spoke no more.

'Can you imagine anything more absurd?' she cried to a friend. 'A man who was my son believes that the Machine is stopping. It would be impious if it was not mad.'

'The Machine is stopping?' her friend replied. 'What does that mean? The phrase conveys nothing to me.'

'Nor to me.'

'He does not refer, I suppose, to the trouble there has been lately with the music?'

'Oh no, of course not. Let us talk about music.'

'Have you complained to the authorities?'

'Yes, and they say it wants mending, and referred me to the Committee of the Mending Apparatus. I complained of those curious gasping sighs that disfigure the symphonies of the Brisbane school. They sound like some one in pain. The Committee of the Mending Apparatus say that it shall be remedied shortly.'

Obscurely worried, she resumed her life. For one thing, the defect in the music irritated her. For another thing, she could not forget Kuno's speech. If he had known that the music was out of repair – he could not know it, for he detested music – if he had known that it was wrong, 'the Machine stops' was exactly the venomous sort of remark he would have made. Of course he had made it at a venture, but the coincidence annoyed her, and she spoke with some petulance to the Committee of the Mending Apparatus.

They replied, as before, that the defect would be set right shortly.

'Shortly! At once!' she retorted. 'Why should I be worried by imperfect music? Things are always put right at once. If you do not mend it at once, I shall complain to the Central Committee.'

'No personal complaints are received by the Central Committee,' the Committee of the Mending Apparatus replied.

'Through whom am I to make my complaint, then?'

'Through us.'

'I complain then.'

'Your complaint shall be forwarded in its turn.'

'Have others complained?'

This question was unmechanical, and the Committee of the Mending Apparatus refused to answer it.

'It is too bad!' she exclaimed to another of her friends. 'There never was such an unfortunate woman as myself. I can never be sure of my music now. It gets worse and worse each time I summon it.'

'I too have my troubles,' the friend replied. 'Sometimes my ideas are interrupted by a slight jarring noise.'

'What is it?'

'I do not know whether it is inside my head, or inside the wall.'

'Complain, in either case.'

'I have complained, and my complaint will be forwarded in its turn to the Central Committee.'

Time passed, and they resented the defects no longer. The defects had not been remedied, but the human tissues in that latter day had become so subservient, that they readily adapted themselves to every caprice of the Machine. The sigh at the crisis of the Brisbane symphony no longer irritated Vashti; she accepted it as part of the melody. The jarring noise, whether in the head or in the wall, was no longer resented by her friend. And so with the mouldy artificial fruit, so with the bath water that began to stink, so with the defective rhymes that the poetry machine had taken to emit. All were bitterly complained of at first, and then acquiesced in and forgotten. Things went from bad to worse unchallenged.

It was otherwise with the failure of the sleeping apparatus. That was a more serious stoppage. There came a day when over the whole world – in Sumatra, in Wessex, in the innumerable cities of Courland and Brazil – the beds, when summoned by their tired owners, failed to appear. It may seem a ludicrous matter, but from it we may date the collapse of humanity. The Committee responsible for the failure was assailed by complainants, whom it referred, as usual, to the Committee of the Mending Apparatus, who in its turn assured them that their complaints would be forwarded to the Central Committee. But the discontent grew, for mankind was not yet sufficiently adaptable to do without sleeping.

'Some one is meddling with the Machine—' they began.

'Some one is trying to make himself king, to reintroduce the personal element.'

'Punish that man with Homelessness.'

'To the rescue! Avenge the Machine! Avenge the Machine!'

'War! Kill the man!'

But the Committee of the Mending Apparatus now came forward, and allayed the panic with well-chosen words. It confessed that the Mending Apparatus was itself in need of repair.

The effect of this frank confession was admirable.

'Of course,' said a famous lecturer – he of the French Revolution, who gilded each new decay with splendour – 'of course we shall not press our complaints now. The Mending Apparatus has treated us so well in the past that we all sympathize with it, and will wait patiently for its recovery. In its own good time it will resume its duties. Meanwhile let us do without our beds, our tabloids, our other little wants. Such, I feel sure, would be the wish of the Machine.'

Thousands of miles away his audience applauded. The Machine still linked them. Under the seas, beneath the roots of the mountains, ran the wires through which they saw and heard, the enormous eyes and ears that were their heritage, and the hum of many workings clothed their thoughts in one garment of subserviency. Only the old and the sick remained ungrateful, for it was rumoured that Euthanasia, too, was out of order, and that pain had reappeared among men.

It became difficult to read. A blight entered the atmosphere and dulled its luminosity. At times Vashti could scarcely see across her room. The air, too, was foul. Loud were the complaints, impotent the remedies, heroic the tone of the lecturer as he cried: 'Courage! courage! What matter so long as the Machine goes on? To it the darkness and the light are one.' And though things improved again after a time, the old brilliancy was never recaptured, and humanity never recovered from its entrance into twilight. There was an hysterical talk of 'measures,' of 'provisional dictatorship,' and the inhabitants of Sumatra were asked to familiarize themselves with the workings of the central power station, the said power station being situated in France. But for the most part panic reigned, and men spent their strength praying to their Books, tangible proofs of the Machine's omnipotence. There were gradations of terror – at times came rumours of hope – the Mending Apparatus was almost mended – the enemies of the Machine had been got under – new 'nerve-centres' were evolving which would do the work even more magnificently than before. But there came a day when, without the slightest warning, without any previous hint of feebleness, the entire communication-system broke down, all over the world, and the world, as they understood it, ended.

Vashti was lecturing at the time and her earlier remarks had been punctuated with applause. As she proceeded the audience became silent, and at the conclusion there was no sound. Somewhat displeased, she called to a friend who was a specialist in sympathy. No sound: doubtless the friend was sleeping. And so with the next friend whom she tried to summon, and so with the next, until she remembered Kuno's cryptic remark, 'The Machine stops.'

The phrase still conveyed nothing. If Eternity was stopping it would of course be set going shortly.

For example, there was still a little light and air – the atmosphere had improved a few hours previously. There was still the Book, and while there was the Book there was security.

Then she broke down, for with the cessation of activity came an unexpected terror – silence.

She had never known silence, and the coming of it nearly killed her – it did kill many thousands of people outright. Ever since her birth she had been surrounded by the steady hum. It was to the ear what artificial air was to the lungs, and agonizing pains shot across her head. And scarcely knowing what she did, she stumbled forward and pressed the unfamiliar button, the one that opened the door of her cell.

Now the door of the cell worked on a simple hinge of its own. It was not connected with the central power station, dying far away in France. It opened, rousing immoderate hopes in Vashti, for she thought that the Machine had been mended. It opened, and she saw the dim tunnel that curved far away towards freedom. One look, and then she shrank back. For the tunnel was full of people – she was almost the last in that city to have taken alarm.

People at any time repelled her, and these were nightmares from her worst dreams. People were crawling about, people were screaming, whimpering, gasping for breath, touching each other, vanishing in the dark, and ever and anon being pushed off the platform on to the live rail. Some were fighting round the electric bells, trying to summon trains which could not be summoned. Others were yelling for Euthanasia or for respirators, or blaspheming the Machine. Others stood at the doors of their cells fearing, like herself, either to stop in them or to leave them. And behind all the uproar was silence—the silence which is the voice of the earth and of the generations who have gone.

No—it was worse than solitude. She closed the door again and sat down to wait for the end. The disintegration went on, accompanied by horrible cracks and rumbling. The valves that restrained the Medical Apparatus must have been weakened, for it ruptured and hung hideously from the ceiling. The floor heaved and fell and flung her from her chair. A tube oozed towards her serpent-fashion. And at last the final horror approached – light began to ebb, and she knew that civilization's long day was closing.

She whirled round, praying to be saved from this, at any rate, kissing the Book, pressing button after button. The uproar outside was increasing, and even penetrated the wall. Slowly the brilliancy of her cell was dimmed, the reflections faded from her metal switches. Now she could not see the reading-stand, now not the Book, though she held it in her hand. Light followed the flight of sound, air was following light, and the original void returned to the cavern from which it had been so long excluded. Vashti continued to whirl, like the devotees of an earlier religion, screaming, praying, striking at the buttons with bleeding hands.

It was thus that she opened her prison and escaped – escaped in the spirit: at least so it seems to me, ere my meditation closes. That she escaped in the body – I cannot perceive that. She struck, by chance, the switch that released the door, and the rush of foul air on her skin, the loud throbbing whispers in her ears, told her that she was facing the tunnel again, and that tremendous platform on which she had seen men fighting. They were not fighting now. Only the whispers remained, and the little whimpering groans. They were dying by hundreds out in the dark.

She burst into tears.

Tears answered her.

They wept for humanity, those two, not for themselves. They could not bear that this should be the end. Ere silence was completed their hearts were opened, and they knew what had been important on the earth. Man, the flower of all flesh, the noblest of all creatures visible, man who had once made god in his image, and had mirrored his strength on the constellations, beautiful naked man was dying, strangled in the garments that he had woven. Century after century had he toiled, and here was his reward. Truly the garment had seemed heavenly at first, shot with the colours of culture, sewn with the threads of self-denial. And heavenly it had been so long as it was a garment and no more, so long as man could shed it at will and live by the essence that is his soul, and the essence, equally divine, that is his body. Then sin against the body – it was for that they wept in chief; the centuries of wrong against the muscles and the nerves, and those five portals by which we can alone apprehend – glazing it over with talk of evolution, until the body was white pap, the home of ideas as colourless, last sloshy stirrings of a spirit that had grasped the stars.

'Where are you?' she sobbed.

His voice in the darkness said, 'Here.'

'Is there any hope, Kuno?'

'None for us.'

'Where are you?'

She crawled towards him over the bodies of the dead. His blood spurted over her hands.

'Quicker,' he gasped, 'I am dying – but we touch, we talk, not through the Machine.'

He kissed her.

'We have come back to our own. We die, but we have recaptured life, as it was in Wessex, when Ælfrid overthrew the Danes. We know what they know outside, they who dwelt in the cloud that is the colour of a pearl.'

'But, Kuno, is it true? Are there still men on the surface of the earth? Is this – this tunnel, this poisoned darkness – really not the end?'

He replied:

'I have seen them, spoken to them, loved them. They are hiding in the mist and the ferns until our civilization stops. To-day they are the Homeless—tomorrow—'

'Oh, tomorrow—some fool will start the Machine again, tomorrow.'

'Never,' said Kuno, 'never. Humanity has learnt its lesson.'

As he spoke, the whole city was broken like a honeycomb. An air-ship had sailed in through the vomitory into a ruined wharf. It crashed downwards, exploding as it went, rending gallery after gallery with its wings of steel. For a moment they saw the nations of the dead, and, before they joined them, scraps of the untainted sky.

Robot AL-76 Goes Astray

ISAAC ASIMOV

Robot AL-76 Goes Astray *first appeared in the February, 1942, issue of* Amazing Stories. *Dr Isaac Asimov (b. 1920), its author, described it as 'blatantly humorous', and so it is. Its humour is as rumbustious as an American film comedy, but it is an interesting example of the 'Let's-be-kind-to-robots' school of science fiction writing begun by Asimov. One is reminded of H. G. Wells's attempt to be kind to ghosts in* The Inexperienced Ghost *at a time when such beings were always ominous and destructive.*

Asimov in 1941 formulated the Three Laws of Robotics, as they are now known: (1) A robot may not injure a human being or through inaction allow a human being to come to harm; (2) A robot must obey the orders given to it by human beings except when such orders would conflict with the First Law; (3) A robot must protect its own existence as long as such protection does not conflict with the First and Second Laws. Robot AL-76 obeys all three.

The word 'robot' first gained currency in the west from its use in the play R.U.R. *(Rossum's Universal Robots) written by Karel Capel in 1921* The Oxford English Dictionary *compares the word with the Polish word 'robotnik', meaning 'a workman'. Asimov himself has pointed out that the original intention of robots was to assist mankind, but soon the creation took over from the creator in the same way that Frankenstein was destroyed by the monster he created in Mary Shelley's novel,* Frankenstein or the Modern Prometheus *(1818). Asimov's robots do not turn on their creators:*

> *'My robots were machines designed by engineers, not pseudo-men created by blasphemers. My robots reacted along the rational lines that existed in their "brains" from the moment of construction. I must admit, though, that occasionally, in my early attempts, I saw the robot as little more than a figure of fun. I pictured it as a completely harmless creature, intent on doing the work for which it was designed. It was incapable of harming men.*

yet it was victimized by human beings who, suffering from a "Frankenstein" complex, insisted on considering the poor machines to be deadly dangerous creatures'

(The Rest of the Robots, 1967, pp. 14–15).

The characters and the language of the story often seem to be making a parody of the 'Western' with its eccentric shack-dweller (Randolph Payne) and his shrewish wife (Mirandy), Sam Tobe of the Petersboro branch of the United States Robot and Mechanical Men Corporation, Sheriff Saunders, Lank Jake, the Deputy, the embattled farmers of Hannaford County, Virginia, and Austin Wilde, the Engineer. The dialogue is often humourously predictable, but the lonely figure of the misunderstood robot stands firmly but forlornly at the centre of the narrative, like the innocent but maligned fugitive in a Western. Man's greed and fear are on trial here, not the machine he has created.

Jonathan Quell's eyes crinkled worriedly behind their rimless glasses as he charged through the door labelled 'General Manager'.

He slapped the folded paper in his hands upon the desk and panted, 'Look at that, boss!'

Sam Tobe juggled the cigar in his mouth from one cheek to the other, and looked. His hand went to his unshaven jaw and rasped along it. 'Hell!' he exploded. 'What are they talking about?'

'They say we sent out five AL robots,' Quell explained, quite unnecessarily.

'We sent six,' said Tobe.

'Sure, six! But they only got five at the other end. They sent out the serial numbers and AL-76 is missing.'

Tobe's chair went over backward as he heaved his thick bulk upright and went through the door as if he were on greased wheels. It was five hours after that – with the plant pulled apart from assembly rooms to vacuum chambers; with every one of the plant's two hundred employees put through the third-degree mill – that a sweating, dishevelled Tobe sent an emergency message to the central plant at Schenectady.

And at the central plant, a sudden explosion of near panic took place. For the first time in the history of the United States Robot and Mechanical Men Corporation, a robot had escaped to the outer world. It wasn't so much that the law forbade the presence of any robot on Earth outside a licensed factory of the corporation. Laws could always be squared. What was much more to the point was the statement made by one of the research mathematicians.

He said: 'That robot was created to run a Disinto on the moon. Its positronic brain was equipped for a lunar environment, and *only* a lunar environment. On Earth it's going to receive seventy-five umptillion sense impressions for which it was never prepared. There's no telling *what* its reactions will be. No telling!' And he wiped a forehead that had suddenly gone wet, with the back of his hand.

Within the hour a stratoplane had left for the Virginia plant. The instructions were simple.

'Get that robot, and get it fast!'

AL-76 was confused! In fact, confusion was the only impression his delicate positronic brain retained. It had started when he had found himself in these strange surroundings. How it had come about, he no longer knew. Everything was mixed up.

There was green under foot, and brown shafts rose all about him with more green on top. And the sky was blue where it should have been black. The sun was all right, round and yellow and hot – but where was the powdery pumice rock underfoot; where were the huge clifflike crater rings?

There was only the green below and the blue above. The sounds that surrounded him were all strange. He had passed through running water that had reached his waist. It was blue and cold and wet. And when he passed people, as he did, occasionally, they were without the space suits they should have been wearing. When they saw him, they shouted and ran.

One man had levelled a gun at him and the bullet had whistled past his head – and then that man had run too.

He had no idea of how long he had been wandering before he finally stumbled upon Randolph Payne's shack two miles out in the woods from the town of Hannaford. Randolph Payne himself – a screwdriver in one hand, a pipe in the other, and a battered ruin of a vacuum cleaner between his knees – squatted outside the doorway.

Payne was humming at the time, for he was a naturally happy-go-lucky soul – when at his shack. He had a more respectable dwelling place back in Hannaford, but *that* dwelling place was pretty largely occupied by his wife, a fact which he silently but sincerely regretted. Perhaps, then, there was a sense of relief and freedom at such times as he found himself able to retire to his 'special deluxe doghouse' where he could smoke in peace and attend to his hobby of reservicing household appliances.

It wasn't much of a hobby, but sometimes someone would bring out a radio or an alarm clock and the money he would get paid for juggling its insides was the only money he ever got that didn't pass in driblets through his spouse's niggardly hands.

This vacuum cleaner, for instance, would bring in an easy six bits.

At the thought he broke into song, raised his eyes, and broke into a sweat. The song choked off, the eyes popped, and the sweat became more intense. He tried to stand up – as a preliminary to running like hell – but he couldn't get his legs to cooperate.

And then AL-76 had squatted down next to him and said, 'Say, why did all the rest of them run?'

Payne knew quite well why they ran, but the gurgle that issued from his diaphragm didn't show it. He tried to inch away from the robot.

AL-76 continued in an aggrieved tone, 'One of them even took a shot at me. An inch lower and he would have scratched my shoulder plate.'

'M-must have b-been a nut,' stammered Payne.

'That's possible.' The robot's voice grew more confidential. 'Listen, what's wrong with everything?'

Payne looked hurriedly about. It had struck him that the robot spoke in a remarkably mild tone for one so heavily and brutally metallic in appearance. It also struck him that he had heard somewhere that robots were mentally incapable of harming human beings. He relaxed a bit.

'There's nothing wrong with anything.'

'Isn't there?' AL-76 eyed him accusingly. '*You're* all wrong. Where's your space suit?'

'I haven't got any.'

'Then why aren't you dead?'

That stopped Payne, "Well – I don't know.'

'See!' said the robot triumphantly, 'there's something wrong with everything. Where's Mount Copernicus? Where's Lunar Station 17? And where's my Disinto? I want to go to work, I do.' He seemed perturbed, and his voice shook as he continued. 'I've been going about for hours trying to get someone to tell me where my

Disinto is, but they all run away. By now I'm probably 'way behind schedule and the Sectional Executive will be as sore as blazes. This is a fine situation.'

Slowly Payne unscrambled the stew in which his brain found itself and said, 'Listen, what do they call you?'

'My serial number is AL-76.'

'All right, Al is good enough for me. Now, Al, if you're looking for Lunar Station 17, that's on the moon, yes?'

AL-76 nodded his head ponderously. 'Sure. But I've been looking for it—'

'But it's on the moon. This isn't the moon.'

It was the robot's turn to become confused. He watched Payne for a speculative moment and then said slowly, 'What do you mean this isn't the moon? Of course it's the moon. Because if it isn't the moon, what is it, huh? Answer me that.'

Payne made a funny sound in his throat and breathed hard. He pointed a finger at the robot and shook it. 'Look,' he said – and then the brilliant idea of the century struck him, and he finished with a strangled 'Wow!'

AL-76 eyed him censoriously. 'That isn't an answer. I think I have a right to a civil answer if I ask a civil question.'

Payne wasn't listening. He was still marvelling at himself. Why, it was as plain as day. This robot was one built for the moon that had somehow got loose on Earth. Naturally it would be all mixed up, because its positronic brain had been geared exclusively for a lunar environment, making its earthly surroundings entirely meaningless.

And now if he could only keep the robot here – until he could get in touch with men at the factory in Petersboro. Why, robots were worth money. The cheapest cost $50,000, he had once heard, and some of them ran into millions. Think of the reward!

Man, oh man, *think of the reward*! And every cent for himself. Not as much as a quarter of a snifter of a plugged nickel for Mirandy. Jumpin' tootin' blazes, *no*!

He rose to his feet at last. 'Al,' he said, 'you and I are buddies! Pals! I love you like a brother.' He thrust out a hand. 'Shake!'

The robot swallowed up the offered hand in a metal paw and squeezed it gently. He didn't quite understand. 'Does that mean you'll tell me how to get to Lunar Station 17?'

Payne was a trifle disconcerted. 'N-no, not exactly. As a matter of fact, I like you so much, I want you to stay here with me awhile.'

'Oh no, I can't do that. I've got to get to work.' He shook his head. 'How would you like to be falling behind your quota hour by hour and minute by minute? I want to work. I've *got* to work.'

Payne thought sourly that there was no accounting for tastes, and said, 'All right, then, I'll explain something to you – because I can see from the looks of you that you're an intelligent person. I've had orders from your Sectional Executive, and he wants me to keep you here for a while. Till he sends for you, in fact.'

'What for?' asked AL-76 suspiciously.

'I can't say. It's secret government stuff.' Payne prayed, inwardly and fervently, that the robot would swallow this. Some robots were clever, he knew, but this looked like one of the early models.

While Payne prayed, AL-76 considered. The robot's brain, adjusted to the handling of a Disinto on the moon, was not at its best when engaged in abstract thought, but just the same, ever since he had got lost, AL-76 had found his thought processes becoming stranger. The alien surroundings did something to him.

His next remark was almost shrewd. He said slyly, 'What's my Sectional Executive's name?'

Payne gulped and thought rapidly. 'Al,' he said in a pained fashion, 'you hurt me with this suspicion. I *can't* tell you his name. The trees have ears.'

AL-76 inspected the tree next to him stolidly and said, 'They have not.'

'I know. What I mean is that spies are all around.'

'Spies?'

'Yes. You know, *bad* people who want to destroy Lunar Station 17.'

'What for?'

'Because they're *bad*. And they want to destroy *you*, and that's why you've got to stay here for a while, so they can't find you.'

'But – but I've got to have a Disinto. I mustn't fall behind my quota.'

'You will have. You will have,' Payne promised earnestly, and just as earnestly damned the robot's one-track mind. 'They're going to send one out tomorrow. Yeah, tomorrow.' That would leave plenty of time to get the men from the factory out here and collect beautiful green heaps of hundred-dollar bills.

But AL-76 grew only the more stubborn under the distressing impingement of the strange world all about him upon his thinking mechanism.

'No,' he said, 'I've got to have a Disinto now.' Stiffly he straightened his joints, jerking erect. 'I'd better look for it some more.'

Payne swarmed after and grabbed a cold, hard elbow. 'Listen,' he squealed, 'You've got to stay—'

And something in the robot's mind clicked. All the strangeness surrounding him collected itself into one globule, exploded, and left a brain ticking with a curiously increased efficiency. He whirled on Payne. 'I tell you what. I can build a Disinto right here – and then I can work it.'

Payne paused doubtfully. 'I don't think I can build one.' He wondered if it would do any good to pretend he could.

'That's all right.' AL-76 could almost feel the positronic paths of his brain weaving into a new pattern, and experienced a strange exhilaration. 'I can build one.' He looked into Payne's deluxe dog-house and said, 'You've got all the material here that I need.'

Randolph Payne surveyed the junk with which his shack was filled: eviscerated radios, a topless refrigerator, rusty automobile engines, a broken-down gas range, several miles of frayed wire, and, taking it all together, fifty tons or thereabouts of the most heterogeneous mass of old metal as ever caused a junkman to sniff disdainfully.

'Have I?' he said weakly.

Two hours later, two things happened practically simultaneously. The first was that Sam Tobe of the Petersboro branch of the United States Robot and Mechanical Men Corporation received a visiphone call from one Randolph Payne of Hannaford. It concerned the missing robot, and Tobe, with a deep-throated snarl, broke connection halfway through and ordered all subsequent calls to be re-routed to the sixth assistant vice-president in charge of buttonholes.

This was not really unreasonable of Tobe. During the past week, although Robot AL-76 had dropped from sight completely, reports had flooded in from all over the Union as to the robot's whereabouts. As many as fourteen a day came – usually from fourteen different states.

Tobe was almighty tired of it, to say nothing of being half crazy on general principles. There was even talk of a Congressional investigation, though every reputable roboticist and mathematical physicist on Earth swore the robot was harmless.

In his state of mind, then, it is not surprising that it took three hours for the general manager to pause and consider just exactly how it was that this Randolph Payne had known that the robot was slated for Lunar Station 17, and, for that matter, how he had known that the robot's serial number was AL-76. Those details had not been given out by the company.

He kept on considering for about a minute and a half and then swung into action.

However, during the three hours between the call and the action, the second event took place. Randolph Payne, having correctly diagnosed the abrupt break in his call as being due to general scepticism on the part of the plant official, returned to his shack with a camera. They couldn't very well argue with a photograph, and he'd be horn-swoggled if he'd show them the real thing before they came across with the cash.

AL-76 was busy with affairs of his own. Half of the contents of Payne's shack was littered over about two acres of ground, and in the middle of it the robot squatted and fooled around with radio tubes, hunks of iron, copper wire, and general junk. He paid no attention to Payne, who, sprawling flat on his belly, focused his camera for a beautiful shot.

And at this point it was that Lemuel Oliver Cooper turned the bend in the road and froze in his tracks as he took in the tableau. The reason for his coming in the first place was an ailing electric toaster that had developed the annoying habit of throwing out pieces of bread forcefully, but thoroughly untoasted. The reason for his *leaving* was more obvious. He had come with a slow, mildly cheerful, spring-morning saunter. He left with a speed that would have caused any college track coach to raise his eyebrows and purse his lips approvingly.

There was no appreciable slackening of speed until Cooper hurtled into Sheriff Saunders' office, minus hat and toaster, and brought himself up hard against the wall.

Kindly hands lifted him, and for half a minute he tried speaking before he had actually calmed down to the point of breathing with, of course, no result.

They gave him whisky and fanned him and when he did speak, it came out something like this: '– monster – seven feet tall – shack all busted up – poor Rannie Payne—' and so on.

They got the story out of him gradually: how there was a huge metal monster, seven feet tall, maybe even eight or nine, out at Randolph Payne's shack; how Randolph Payne himself was on his stomach, a 'poor, bleeding, mangled corpse'; how the monster was then busily engaged in wrecking the shack out of sheer destructiveness; how it had turned on Lemuel Oliver Cooper, and how he, Cooper, had made his escape by half a hair.

Sheriff Saunders hitched his belt tighter about his portly middle and said, 'It's that there machine man that got away from the Petersboro factory. We got warning on it last Saturday. Hey, Jake, you get every man in Hannaford County that can shoot and slap a deputy's badge on him. Get them here at noon. And listen, Jake, before you do that, just drop in at the Widow Payne's place and tell her the bad news gentle-like.'

It is reported that Miranda Payne, upon being acquainted with events, paused only to make sure that her husband's insurance policy was safe, and to make a few pithy remarks concerning her foolishness in not having had him take out double the amount, before breaking out into as prolonged and heart-wringing a wail of grief as ever became a respectable widow.

It was some hours later that Randolph Payne – unaware of his horrible mutilation and death – viewed the completed negatives of his snapshots with satisfaction. As a series of portraits of a robot at work, they left nothing to the imagination. They might have been labelled: 'Robot Gazing Thoughtfully at Vacuum Tube,' 'Robot Splicing Two Wires,' 'Robot Wielding Screwdriver,' 'Robot Taking Refrigerator Apart with Great Violence,' and so on.

As there now remained only the routine of making the prints themselves, he stepped out from beyond the curtain of the improvised darkroom for a bit of a smoke and a chat with AL-76.

In doing so, he was blissfully unaware that the neighbouring woods were verminous with nervous farmers armed with anything from an old colonial relic of a blunderbuss to the portable machine gun carried by the sheriff himself. Nor, for that matter, had he any inkling of the fact that half a dozen roboticists, under the leadership of Sam Tobe, were smoking down the highway from Petersboro at better than a hundred and twenty miles an hour for the sole purpose of having the pleasure and honour of his acquaintance.

So while things were jittering toward a climax, Randolph Payne sighed with self-satisfaction, lighted a match upon the seat of his pants, puffed away at his pipe, and looked at AL-76 with amusement.

It had been apparent for quite some time that the robot was more than slightly lunatic. Randolph Payne was himself an expert at home-made contraptions, having built several that could not have been exposed to daylight without searing the eyeballs of all beholders; but he had never even conceived of anything approaching the monstrosity that AL-76 was concocting.

It would have made the Rube Goldbergs of the day die in convulsions of envy. It would have made Picasso (if he could have lived to witness it) quit art in the sheer knowledge that he had been hopelessly surpassed. It would have soured the milk in the udders of any cow within half a mile.

In fact, it was gruesome!

From a rusty and massive iron base that faintly resembled something Payne had once seen attached to a secondhand tractor, it rose upward in rakish, drunken swerves through a bewildering mess of wires, wheels, tubes, and nameless horrors without number, ending in a megaphone arrangement that looked decidedly sinister.

Payne had the impulse to peek in the megaphone part, but refrained. He had seen far more sensible machines explode suddenly and with violence.

He said, 'Hey, Al.'

The robot looked up. He had been lying flat on his stomach, teasing a thin sliver of metal into place. 'What do you want, Payne?'

'What is this?' He asked it in the tone of one referring to something foul and decomposing, held gingerly between two ten-foot poles.

'It's the Disinto I'm making – so I can start to work. It's an improvement on the standard model.' The robot rose, dusted his knees clankingly, and looked at it proudly.

Payne shuddered. An 'improvement'! No wonder they hid the original in caverns on the moon. Poor satellite! Poor dead satellite! He had always wanted to know what a fate worse than death was. Now he knew.

'Will it work?' he asked.

'Sure.'

'How do you know?'

'It's got to. I made it, didn't I? I only need one thing now. Got a flashlight?'

'Somewhere, I guess.' Payne vanished into the shack and returned almost immediately.

The robot unscrewed the bottom and set to work. In five minutes he had finished. He stepped back and said, 'All set. Now I get to work. You may watch if you want to.'

A pause, while Payne tried to appreciate the magnanimity of the offer. 'Is it safe?'

'A baby could handle it.'

'Oh!' Payne grinned weakly and got behind the thickest tree in the vicinity. 'Go ahead,' he said, 'I have the utmost confidence in you.'

AL-76 pointed to the nightmarish junk pile and said, 'Watch!' His hands set to work—

The embattled farmers of Hannaford County, Virginia, weaved up upon Payne's shack in a slowly tightening circle. With the blood of their heroic colonial forebears pounding their veins – and goose flesh trickling up and down their spines – they crept from tree to tree.

Sheriff Saunders spread the word. 'Fire when I give the signal – and aim at the eyes.'

Jacob Linker – Lank Jake to his friends, and Sheriff's Deputy to himself – edged close. 'You think maybe this machine man has skedaddled?' He did not quite manage to suppress the tone of wistful hopefulness in his voice.

'Dunno,' grunted the sherriff. 'Guess not, though. We woulda come across him in the woods if he had, and we haven't.'

'But it's awful quiet, and it appears to me as if we're getting close to Payne's place.'

The reminder wasn't necessary. Sheriff Saunders had a lump in his throat so big it had to be swallowed in three instalments. 'Get back,' he ordered, 'and keep your finger on the trigger.'

They were at the rim of the clearing now, and Sheriff Saunders closed his eyes and stuck the corner of one out from behind the tree. Seeing nothing, he paused, then tried again, eyes open this time.

Results were, naturally, better.

To be exact, he saw one huge machine man, back toward him, bending over one soul-curdling, hiccupy contraption of uncertain origin and less certain purpose. The only item he missed was the quivering figure of Randolph Payne, embracing the tree next but three to the nor'-nor'west.

Sheriff Saunders stepped out into the open and raised his machine gun. The robot, still presenting a broad metal back, said in a loud voice – to person or persons unknown – 'Watch!' and as the sheriff opened his mouth to signal a general order to fire, metal fingers compressed a switch.

There exists no adequate description of what occurred afterward, in spite of the presence of seventy eyewitnesses. In the days, months, and years to come not one of those seventy ever had a word to say about the few seconds after the sheriff had opened his mouth to give the firing order. When questioned about it, they merely turned apple-green and staggered away.

It is plain from circumstantial evidence, however, that, in a general way, what did occur was this.

Sheriff Saunders opened his mouth; AL-76 pulled a switch. The Disinto worked, and seventy-five trees, two barns, three cows and the top three quarters of Duckbill Mountain whiffed into rarefied atmosphere. They became, so to speak, one with the snows of yesteryear.

Sheriff Saunders' mouth remained open for an indefinite interval thereafter, but nothing – neither firing orders nor anything else – issued therefrom. And then—

And then, there was a stirring in the air, a multiple ro-o-o-oshing sound, a series of purple streaks through the atmosphere radiating away from Randolph Payne's shack as the centre, and of the members of the posse, not a sign.

There were various guns scattered about the vicinity, including the sheriff's patented nickel-plated, extra-rapid-fire, guaranteed-no-clog, portable machine gun. There were about fifty hats, a few half-chomped cigars, and some odds and ends that had come loose in the excitement – but of actual human beings there was none.

Except for Lank Jake, not one of those human beings came within human ken for three days, and the exception in his favour came about because he was interrupted in his comet-flight by the half-dozen men from the Petersboro factory, who were charging *into* the wood at a pretty fair speed of their own.

It was Sam Hobe who stopped him, catching Lank Jake's head skilfully in the pit of his stomach. When he caught his breath, Tobe asked, 'Where's Randolph Payne's place?'

Lank Jake allowed his eyes to unglaze for just a moment. 'Brother,' he said, 'just you follow the direction I ain't going.'

And with that, miraculously, he was gone. There was a shrinking dot dodging trees on the horizon that might have been he, but Sam Tobe wouldn't have sworn to it.

That takes care of the posse; but there still remains Randolph Payne, whose reactions took something of a different form.

For Randolph Payne, the five-second interval after the pulling of the switch and the disappearance of Duckbill Mountain was a total blank. At the start he had been peering through the thick underbrush from behind the bottom of the trees; at the end he was swinging wildly from one of the topmost branches. The same impulse that had driven the posse horizontally had driven him vertically.

As to how he had covered the fifty feet from roots to top – whether he had climbed, jumped, or flown – he did not know, and he didn't give a particle of never-mind.

What he *did* know was that property had been destroyed by a robot temporarily in his possession. All visions of rewards vanished and were replaced by trembling nightmares of hostile citizenry, shrieking lynch mobs, lawsuits, murder charges, and what Mirandy Payne would say. Mostly what Mirandy Payne would say.

He was yelling wildly and hoarsely, 'Hey, you robot, you smash that thing, do you hear? Smash it good! You forget I ever had anything to do with it? You're a stranger to me, see? You don't ever say a word about it. Forget it, you hear?'

He didn't expect his orders to do any good; it was only reflex action. What he didn't know was that a robot always obeys a human order except where carrying it out involves danger to another human.

AL-76, therefore, calmly and methodically proceeded to demolish his Disinto.

Just as he was stamping the last cubic inch under foot, Sam Tobe and his contingent arrived, and Raldolph Payne, sensing that the real owners of the robot had come, dropped out of the tree head-first and made for regions unknown feet-first.

He did not wait for his reward.

Austin Wilde, Robotical Engineer, turned to Sam Tobe and said, 'Did you get anything out of the robot?'

Tobe shook his head and snarled deep in his throat. 'Nothing. Not one thing. He's forgotten everything that's happened since he left the factory. He must have gotten *orders* to forget, or it couldn't have left him so blank. What was that pile of junk he'd been fooling with?'

'Just that. A pile of junk! But it must have been a Disinto before he smashed it, and I'd like to kill the fellow who ordered him to smash it – by slow torture, if possible. Look at this !'

They were part of the way up the slopes of what had been Duckbill Mountain – at that point, to be exact, where the top had been sheered off; and Wilde put his hand down upon the perfect flatness that cut through both soil and rock.

'*What* a Disinto !' he said. 'It took the mountain right off its base.'

'What made him build it?'

Wilde shrugged. 'I don't know. Some factor in his environment – there's no way of knowing what – reacted upon his moon-type positronic brain to produce a Disinto out of junk. It's a billion to one against our ever stumbling upon that factor again now that the robot himself has forgotten. We'll never have that Disinto.'

'Never mind. The important thing is that we have the robot.'

'The hell you say.' There was poignant regret in Wilde's voice. 'Have you ever had anything to do with the Disintos on the moon? They eat up energy like so many electronic hogs and won't even begin to run until you've built up a potential of better than a million volts. But *this* Disinto worked differently. I went through the rubbish with a microscope, and would you like to see the only source of power of any kind that I found?'

'What was it?'

'Just this ! And we'll never know how he did it.'

And Austin Wilde held up the source of power that had enabled a Disinto to chew up a mountain in half a second – *two flashlight batteries* !

Compassion Circuit

JOHN WYNDHAM

John Wyndham was one of the pseudonyms under which John Beynon Harris (1903–1969) wrote. He was educated at Bedales and then tried his hand at farming, law, commercial art and advertising. He is best known for his science fiction novels, such as The Day of the Triffids, The Kraken Wakes, The Chrysalids, *and* The Midwich Cuckoos.

His short story Compassion Circuit *is in marked contrast to Asimov's* Robot AL-76 Goes Astray; *it is in the 'Frankenstein' tradition of the created monster (or machine) which reacts against the creator and, more ominously, here takes over his body to create a robot of him. In Wyndham's story, too, the robot acts out of kindness – Hester thinks that what she does is for the best, even if it means changing the very physical nature of both Janet and George. The robot sees the weakness of Janet's body as inefficiency and clumsiness.*

The domesticity of George's life indicates the reader's starting point, the position which he understands and with which he can identify. The fact that George accepts robots and their work helps the reader to suspend his own disbelief. It is ironic that the one measure taken by humans to ensure that robots do not run wild – the compassion circuit – is the very thing which ultimately causes the destruction of their own human nature. Perhaps Man's own compassion is the weakness in his make-up which leads him to impose his will on others for their own good, but which destroys himself in the end. Wyndham leaves the reader to make his own comment.

By the time Janet had been five days in hospital she had become converted to the idea of a domestic robot. It had taken her two days to discover that Nurse James *was* a robot, one day to get over the surprise, and two more to realize what a comfort an attendant robot could be.

The conversion was a relief. Practically every house she visited had a domestic robot; it was the family's second or third most valuable possession – the women tended to rate it slightly higher than the car; the men, slightly lower. Janet had been perfectly well aware for some time that her friends regarded her as a nitwit or worse for wearing herself out with looking after a house which a robot would be able to keep spick and span with a few hours' work a day. She had also known that it irritated George to come home each evening to a wife who had tired herself out by unnecessary work. But the prejudice had been firmly set. It was not the diehard attitude of people who refused to be served by robot waiters, or driven by robot drivers (who, incidentally, were much safer), led by robot shop-guides, or see dresses modelled by robot mannequins. It was simply an uneasiness about them, and being left alone with one – and a disinclination to feel such an uneasiness in her own home.

She herself attributed the feeling largely to the conservatism of her own home which had used no house-robots. Other people, who had been brought up in homes run by robots, even the primitive types available a generation before, never seemed to have such a feeling at all. It irritated her to know that her husband thought she was *afraid* of them in a childish way. That, she had explained to George a number of times, was not so, and was not the point, either: what she did dislike was the idea of one intruding upon her personal, domestic life, which was what a house-robot was bound to do.

The robot who was called Nurse James was, then, the first with which she had ever been in close personal contact and she, or it, came as a revelation.

Janet told the doctor of her enlightenment, and he looked relieved. She also told George when he looked in in the afternoon: he was delighted. The two of them conferred before he left the hospital.

'Excellent,' said the doctor. 'To tell you the truth I was afraid we were up against a real neurosis there – and very inconveniently, too. Your wife can never have been strong, and in the last few years she's worn herself out running the house.'

'I know,' George agreed. 'I tried hard to persuade her during the first two years we were married, but it only led to trouble so I had to drop it. This is really a culmination – she was rather shaken when she found that the reason she'd have to come here was partly because there was no robot at home to look after her.'

'Well, there's one thing certain, she can't go on as she has been doing. If she tries to she'll be back here inside a couple of months,' the doctor told him.

'She won't know. She's really changed her mind,' George assured him. 'Part of the trouble was that she's never come across a really modern one, except in a superficial way. The newest that any of our friends has is ten years old at least, and most of them are older than that. She'd never contemplated the idea of anything as advanced as Nurse James. The question now is what pattern?'

The doctor thought a moment.

'Frankly, Mr Shand, your wife is going to need a lot of rest and looking after, I'm afraid. What I'd really recommend for her is the type they have here. It's something pretty new, this Nurse James model. A specially developed high-sensibility job with a quite novel contra-balanced compassion-protection circuit – a very tricky bit of work that. Any direct order which a normal robot would obey at once is evaluated by the circuit, it is weighed against the benefit or harm to the patient and, unless it is beneficial, or at least harmless, to the patient, it is not obeyed. They've proved to be wonderful for nursing and looking after children – but there is a big demand for them, and I'm afraid they're pretty expensive.'

'How much?' asked George.

The doctor's round-figure price made him frown for a moment. Then he said: 'It'll make a hole, but, after all, it's mostly Janet's economies and simple-living that's built up the savings. Where do I get one?'

'You don't. Not just like that,' the doctor told him. 'I shall have to throw a bit of weight about for a priority, but in the circumstances I shall get it, all right. Now, you go and fix up the details of appearance and so on with your wife. Let me know how she wants it, and I'll get busy.'

'A proper one,' said Janet. 'One that'll look right in a house, I mean, I couldn't do with one of those levers-and-plastic box things that stare at you with lenses. As it's got to look after the house, let's have it looking like a housemaid.'

'Or a houseman, if you like?'

She shook her head. 'No. It's going to have to look after me, too, so I think I'd rather it was a housemaid. It can have a black silk dress and a frilly white apron and a cap. And I'd like it blonde – a sort of darkish blonde – and about five feet ten, and nice to look at, but not too beautiful. I don't want to be jealous of it. . . .'

The doctor kept Janet ten days more in the hospital while the matter was settled. There had been luck in coming in for a cancelled order, but inevitably some delay while it was adapted to Janet's specification – also it had required the addition of standard domestic pseudo-memory patterns to suit it for housework.

It was delivered the day after she got back. Two severely functional robots carried the case up the front path, and inquired whether they should unpack it. Janet thought not, and told them to leave it in the outhouse.

When George got back he wanted to open it at once, but Janet shook her head.

'Supper first,' she decided. 'A robot doesn't mind waiting.'

Nevertheless it was a brief meal. When it was over, George carried the dishes out and stacked them in the sink.

'No more washing-up,' he said, with satisfaction.

He went out to borrow the next-door robot to help him carry the case in. Then he found his end of it more than he could lift, and had to borrow the robot from the house opposite, too. Presently the pair of them carried it in and laid it on the kitchen floor as if it were a featherweight, and went away again.

George got out the screwdriver and drew the six large screws that held the lid down. Inside there was a mass of shavings. He shoved them out, on to the floor. Janet protested.

'What's the matter? *We* shan't have to clear up,' he said, happily.

There was an inner case of wood pulp, with a snowy layer of wadding under its lid. George rolled it up and pushed it out of the way, and there, ready dressed in black frock and white apron, lay the robot.

They regarded it for some seconds without speaking.

It was remarkably lifelike. For some reason it made Janet feel a little queer to realize that it was *her* robot – a trifle nervous, and, obscurely, a trifle guilty. . . .

'Sleeping beauty,' remarked George, reaching for the instruction book on its chest.

In point of fact the robot was not a beauty. Janet's preference had been observed. It was pleasant and nice-looking without being striking, but the details were good. The deep gold hair was quite enviable – although one knew that it was probably threads of plastic with waves that would never come out. The skin – another kind of plastic covering the carefully built-up contours – was distinguishable from real skin only by its perfection.

Janet knelt down beside the box, and ventured a forefinger to touch the flawless complexion. It was quite, quite cold.

She sat back on her heels, looking at it. Just a big doll, she told herself; a contraption, a very wonderful contraption of metal, plastics, and electronic circuits, but still a contraption, and made to look as it did simply because people, including herself, would find it harsh or grotesque if it should look any other way. . . . And yet, to have it looking as it did was a bit disturbing, too. For one thing, you couldn't go on thinking of it as 'it' any more; whether you liked it or not, your mind thought of it as 'her'. As 'her' it would have to have a name; and, with a name, it would become still more of a person.

' "A battery-driven model," ' George read out, ' "will normally require to be fitted with a new battery every four days. Other models, however, are designed to conduct their own regeneration from the mains as and when necessary." Let's have her out.'

He put his hands under the robot's shoulders, and tried to lift it. 'Phew!' he said. 'Must be about three times my weight.' He had another try. 'Hell,' he said, and referred to the book again.

' "The control switches are situated at the back, slightly above the waistline." All right, maybe we can roll her over.'

With an effort he succeeded in getting the figure on to its side and began to undo the buttons at the back of her dress. Janet suddenly felt that to be an indelicacy. 'I'll do it,' she said.

Her husband glanced at her.

'All right. It's yours,' he told her.

'She can't be just "it". I'm going to call her Hester.'

'All right, again,' he agreed.

Janet undid the buttons and fumbled about inside the dress.

'I can't find the knob, or anything,' she said.

'Apparently there's a small panel that opens,' he told her.

'Oh, no!' she said, in a slightly shocked tone.

He regarded her again,

'Darling, she's just a robot; a mechanism.'

'I know,' said Janet, shortly. She felt about again, discovered the panel, and opened it.

'You give the upper knob a half-turn to the right and then close the panel to complete the circuit,' instructed George, from the book.

Janet did so, and then sat swiftly back on her heels again, watching.

The robot stirred and turned. It sat up, then it got to its feet. It stood before them, looking the very pattern of a stage parlourmaid. 'Good day, madam,' it said. 'Good day, sir. I shall be happy to serve you.'

'Thank you, Hester,' Janet said, as she leaned back against the cushion placed behind her. Not that it was necessary to thank a robot, but she had a theory that if you did not practise politeness with robots you soon forgot it with other people.

And, anyway, Hester was no ordinary robot. She was not even dressed as a parlourmaid any more. In four months she had become a friend, a tireless, attentive friend. From the first Janet had found it difficult to believe that she was only a mechanism, and as the days passed she had become more and more of a person. The fact that she consumed electricity instead of food came to seem little more than a foible. The time she couldn't stop walking in a circle, and the other time when something went wrong with her vision so that she did everything a foot to the right of where she ought to have been doing it, these things were just indispositions such as anyone might have, and the robot-mechanic who came to adjust her paid his call much like any other doctor. Hester was not only a person; she was preferable company to many.

'I suppose,' said Janet, settling back in her chair, 'that you must think me a poor, weak thing?'

What one must not expect from Hester was euphemism.

'Yes,' she said, directly. But then she added: 'I think all humans are poor, weak things. It is the way they are made. One must be sorry for them.'

Janet had long ago given up thinking things like: 'That'll be the compassion circuit speaking,' or trying to imagine the computing, selecting, associating, and shunting that must be going on to produce such a remark. She took it as she might from – well, say, a foreigner. She said:

'Compared with robots we must seem so, I suppose. You are so strong and untiring, Hester. If you knew how I envy you that. . . .'

Hester said, matter of factly: 'We were designed: you were just accidental. It is your misfortune, not your fault.'

'You'd rather be you than me?' asked Janet.

'Certainly,' Hester told her. 'We are stronger. We don't have to have frequent sleep to recuperate. We don't have to carry an unreliable chemical factory inside us. We don't have to grow old and deteriorate. Human beings are so clumsy and fragile and so often unwell because something is not working properly. If anything goes wrong with us, or is broken, it doesn't hurt and is easily replaced. And you have all kinds of words like pain, and suffering, and unhappiness, and weariness that we have to be taught to understand, and they don't seem to us to be useful things to have. I feel very sorry that you must have these things and be so uncertain and so fragile. It disturbs my compassion-circuit.'

'Uncertain and fragile,' Janet repeated. 'Yes, that's how I feel.'

'Humans have to live so precariously,' Hester went on. 'If my arm or leg should be crushed I can have a new one in a few minutes, but a human would have agony for a long time, and not even a new limb at the end of it – just a faulty one, if he is lucky. That isn't as bad as it used to be because in designing us you learned how to make good arms and legs, much stronger and better than the old ones. People would be much more sensible to have a weak arm or leg replaced at once, but they don't seem to want to if they can possibly keep the old ones.'

'You mean they can be grafted on? I didn't know that,' Janet said. 'I wish it were only arms or legs that's wrong with me. I don't think I would hesitate. . . .' She sighed. 'The doctor wasn't encouraging this morning, Hester. You heard what he said? I've been losing ground: must rest more. I don't believe he does expect me to get any stronger. He was just trying to cheer me up before. . . . He had a funny sort of look after he'd examined me. . . . But all he said was rest. What's the good of being alive if it's only rest – rest – rest. . . ? And there's poor George. What sort of life is it for him, and he's so patient with me, so sweet. . . . I'd rather anything than go on feebly like this. I'd sooner die. . . .'

Janet went on talking, more to herself than to the patient Hester standing by. She talked herself into tears. Then, presently, she looked up.

'Oh, Hester, if you were human I couldn't bear it; I think I'd hate you for being so strong and so well – but I don't, Hester. You're so kind and so patient when I'm silly, like this. I believe you'd cry with me to keep me company if you could.'

'I would if I could,' the robot agreed. 'My compassion-circuit—'

'Oh, *no*!' Janet protested. 'It can't be just that. You've a heart somewhere, Hester. You must have.'

'I expect it is more reliable than a heart,' said Hester.

She stepped a little closer, stooped down, and lifted Janet up as if she weighed nothing at all.

'You've tired yourself out, Janet, dear,' she told her. 'I'll take you upstairs; you'll be able to sleep a little before he gets back.'

Janet could feel the robot's arms cold through her dress, but the coldness did not trouble her any more, she was aware only that they were strong, protecting arms around her. She said:

'Oh, Hester, you are such a comfort, you *know* what I ought to do.' She paused, then she added miserably: 'I know what he thinks – the doctor, I mean. I could see it. He just thinks I'm going to go on getting weaker and weaker until one day I'll fade away and die. . . . I said I'd sooner die . . . but I wouldn't, Hester. I don't want to die. . . .'

The robot rocked her a little, as if she were a child.

'There, there, dear. It's not as bad as that – nothing like,' she told her. 'You mustn't think about dying. And you mustn't cry any more, it's not good for you, you know. Besides, you don't want him to see you've been crying.'

'I'll try not to,' agreed Janet obediently, as Hester carried her out of the room and up the stairs.

The hospital reception-robot looked up from the desk.

'My wife,' George said, 'I rang you up about an hour ago.'

The robot's face took on an impeccable expression of professional sympathy.

'Yes, Mr Shand. I'm afraid it has been a shock for you, but as I told you, your house-robot did quite the right thing to send her here at once.'

'I've tried to get on to her own doctor, but he's away,' George told her.

'You don't need to worry about that, Mr Shand. She has been examined, and we have had all her records sent over from the hospital she was in before. The operation has been provisionally fixed for tomorrow, but of course we shall need your consent.'

George hesitated. 'May I see the doctor in charge of her?'

'He isn't in the hospital at the moment, I'm afraid.'

'Is it – absolutely necessary?' George asked after a pause.

The robot looked at him steadily, and nodded.

'She must have been growing steadily weaker for some months now,' she said. George nodded.

'The only alternative is that she will grow weaker still, and have more pain before the end,' she told him.

George stared at the wall blankly for some seconds.

'I see,' he said bleakly.

He picked up a pen in a shaky hand and signed the form that she put before him. He gazed at it a while without seeing it.

'She'll – she'll have – a good chance?' he asked.

'Yes,' the robot told him. 'There is never complete absence of risk, of course, but she has a better than seventy-per-cent likelihood of complete success.'

George sighed, and nodded. 'I'd like to see her,' he said.

The robot pressed a bell-push.

'You may *see* her,' she said. 'But I must ask you not to disturb her. She's asleep now, and it's better for her not to be woken.'

George had to be satisfied with that, but he left the hospital feeling a little better for the sight of the quiet smile on Janet's lips as she slept.

The hospital called him at the office the following afternoon. They were reassuring. The operation appeared to have been a complete success. Everyone was quite confident of the outcome. There was no need to worry. The doctors were perfectly satisfied. No, it would not be wise to allow any visitors for a few days yet. But there was nothing to worry about. Nothing at all.

George rang up each day just before he left, in the hope that he would be allowed a visit. The hospital was kindly and heartening, but adamant about visits. And then, on the fifth day, they suddenly told him she had left on her way home. George was staggered: he had been prepared to find it a matter of weeks. He dashed out, bought a bunch of roses, and left half a dozen traffic regulations in fragments behind him. 'Where is she?' he demanded of Hester as she opened the door.

'She's in bed. I thought it might be better if—' Hester began, but he lost the rest of the sentence as he bounded up the stairs.

Janet was lying in the bed. Only her head was visible, cut off by the line of the sheet and a bandage round her neck. George put the flowers down on the bedside table. He stooped over Janet and kissed her gently. She looked up at him from anxious eyes.

'Oh, George dear. Has she told you?'

'Has who told me what?' he asked, sitting down on the side of the bed.

'Hester. She said she would. Oh, George, I didn't mean it, at least I don't think I meant it. . . . She sent me, George. I was so weak and wretched. I wanted to be strong. I don't think I really understood. Hester said—'

'Take it easy, darling. Take it easy,' George suggested with a smile. 'What on earth's all this about?'

He felt under the bedclothes and found her hand.

'But, George—' she began. He interrupted her.

'I say, darling, your hand's dreadfully cold. It's almost like—' His fingers slid further up her arm. His eyes widened at her, incredulously. He jumped up suddenly from the bed and flung back the covers. He put his hand on the thin nightdress, over her heart – and then snatched it away as if he had been stung. 'God – NO!—' he said, staring at her.

'But George. George darling—' said Janet's head on the pillows.

'NO – NO!' cried George, almost in a shriek.

He turned and ran blindly from the room.

In the darkness on the landing he missed the top step of the stairs, and went headlong down the whole flight.

Hester found him lying in a huddle in the hall. She bent down gently and explored the damage. The extent of it, and the fragility of the frame that had suffered it disturbed her compassion-circuit very greatly. She did not try to move him, but went to the telephone and dialled.

'Emergency?' she asked, and gave the name and address. 'Yes, at once,' she told them. 'There may not be a lot of time. Several compound fractures, and I think his back is broken, poor man. No. There appears to be no damage to his head. Yes, much better. He'd be crippled for life, even if he did get over it . . . . Yes, better send the form of consent with the ambulance so that it can be signed at once. . . . Oh, yes, that'll be quite all right. His wife will sign it.'

Expedition to Earth

ARTHUR C. CLARKE

Arthur C. Clarke (b. 1917), one of the most accomplished writers of modern science fiction, became a specialist in radar whilst in the RAF during the Second World War. In 1948 he graduated from the University of London with a degree in Physics and then became an assistant editor of Science Abstracts. *For a time he served as Chairman of the British Interplanetary Society.*

Expedition to Earth *(published in 1954) is a 'visit-by-aliens' science fiction story, but it is much more; it is ingenious in its twists and very skilful in its composition. The narrative is anchored in the present for the reader by references which he can understand and recognize; indeed, it depends for its effect on seeing that a Hollywood cartoon may embody many of the values for which our society seems to stand. The science fiction writer is acting once more as the satirist. The story moves rapidly forward to a time centuries ahead where Man is fighting – and losing – his battle against the forces of Nature, but ironically the very changes in the universe which destroy Man create life on Venus. The conclusion then moves further forward to a time 5000 years on when the Venusians have advanced sufficiently to visit Earth.*

Time-shifts, the struggle against hostile climatic conditions, reptilian aliens are familiar enough elements of science fiction now. Clarke's composition, like Swift's in Gulliver's Travels, *allows comments to be made about our own civilization. What are the things by which we shall be judged by posterity? How far will future generations be able to reconcile our ability to make technological advances with our love for – or, at least, toleration of – warfare? The Venusians say incredulously, 'Some philosophers maintain that knowledge of machinery does not necessarily imply a high degree of civilization, and it is theoretically possible to have wars in a society possessing mechanical power, flight, and even radio. Such a conception is very alien to our thoughts, but we must admit its possibility.'*

It is this underlying seriousness in the story set off against its fundamental humour which gives it its 'bite'. The aliens treat the cartoon with a real scientific intenseness and as they are reptilian they invert our science fiction writer's views of life on other planets in a delightfully ironic fashion:

> *'For centuries our artists have been depicting scenes from the history of the dead world, peopling it with all manner of fantastic beings. Most of the creations have resembled us more or less closely, though it has often been pointed out that because we are reptiles it does not follow that all intelligent life must necessarily be reptilian.'*

Expedition to Earth *shows, too, Arthur Clarke's ability to describe landscape economically, but deftly and surely. Some of these descriptions have, perhaps, been turned into clichés in the cinema and on the television screen, but Clarke's achievement in 1954 was none the less because of that. The famous Western* High Noon, *with its tense final confrontation in a dusty street, has been similarly treated and its situations clichéd, but none would deny its achievement in the development of its own art form.*

No one could remember when the tribe had begun its long journey: the land of great rolling plains that had been its first home was now no more than a half-forgotten dream. For many years Shann and his people had been fleeing through a country of low hills and sparkling lakes, and now the mountains lay ahead. This summer they must cross them to the southern lands, and there was little time to lose.

The white terror that had come down from the poles, grinding continents to dust and freezing the very air before it, was less than a day's march behind. Shann wondered if the glaciers could climb the mountains ahead, and within his heart he dared to kindle a little flame of hope. They might prove a barrier against which even the remorseless ice would batter in vain. In the southern lands of which the legends spoke, his people might find refuge at last.

It took many weeks to discover a pass through which the tribe and its animals could travel. When midsummer came, they had camped in a lonely valley where the air was thin and the stars shone with a brilliance none had ever seen before. The summer was waning when Shann took his two sons and went ahead to explore the way. For three days they climbed, and for three nights slept as best they could on the freezing rocks. And on the fourth morning there was nothing ahead but a gentle rise to a cairn of grey stones built by other travellers, centuries ago.

Shann felt himself trembling, and not with cold, as they walked towards the little pyramid of stones. His sons had fallen behind; no one spoke, for too much was at stake. In a little while they would know if all their hopes had been betrayed.

To east and west, the wall of mountains curved away as if embracing the land beneath. Below lay endless miles of undulating plain, with a great river swinging across it in tremendous loops. It was fertile land; one in which the tribe could raise its crops knowing that there would be no need to flee before the harvest came.

Then Shann lifted his eyes to the south, and saw the doom of all his hopes. For there, at the edge of the world, glimmered that deadly light he had seen so often to the north – the glint of ice below the horizon.

There was no way forward. Through all the years of flight, the glaciers from the south had been advancing to meet them. Soon they would be crushed beneath the moving walls of ice—

The southern glaciers did not reach the mountains until a generation later. In that last summer, the sons of Shann carried the sacred treasures of the tribe to the lonely cairn overlooking the plain. The ice that had once gleamed below the horizon was now almost at their feet; by the spring it would be splintering against the mountain walls.

No one understood the treasures, now: they were from a past too distant for the understanding of any man alive. Their origins were lost in the mists that surrounded the Golden Age, and how they had come at last into the possession of this wandering tribe was a story that now never would be told. For it was the story of a civilization that had passed beyond recall.

Once, all these pitiful relics had been treasured for some good reason and now they had become sacred, though their meaning had long been lost. The print in the old books had faded centuries ago, though much of the lettering was still readable – if there had been any to read it. But many generations had passed since anyone had had a use for a set of seven-figure logarithms, an atlas of the world, and the score of Sibelius's Seventh Symphony printed, according to the flyleaf, by H. K. Chu & Sons at the City of Pekin in the year AD 2021.

The old books were placed reverently in the little crypt that had been made to receive them. There followed a motley collection of fragments: gold and platinum coins, a broken telephoto lens, a watch, a cold-light lamp, a microphone, the cutter from an electric shaver, some midget radio valves – the flotsam that had been left behind when the great tide of civilization ebbed for ever. All these were carefully stowed away in their resting-place. Then came three more relics, the most sacred of all because the least understood.

The first was a strangely shaped piece of metal, showing the coloration of intense heat. It was, in its way, the most pathetic of all these symbols from the past, for it told of Man's greatest achievement and of the future he might have known. The mahogany stand on which it was mounted bore a silver plate with the inscription:

Auxiliary igniter from starboard jet of spaceship
Morning Star, Earth–Moon, AD 1985

Next followed another miracle of the ancient science: a sphere of transparent plastic with oddly shaped pieces of metal embedded in it. At its centre was a tiny capsule of synthetic radio-element, surrounded by the converting screens that shifted its radiation far down the spectrum. As long as the material remained active, the sphere would be a tiny radio transmitter broadcasting power in all directions. Only a few of these spheres had ever been made; they had been designed as perpetual beacons to mark the orbits of the Asteroids. But Man had never reached the Asteroids, and the beacons had never been used.

Last of all was a flat circular tin, very wide in comparison to its depth. It was heavily sealed, and rattled when it was shaken. The tribal lore predicted that disaster would follow if it were ever opened, and no one knew that it held one of the great works of art of nearly a thousand years before.

The work was finished. The two men rolled the stones back into place and slowly began to descend the mountainside. Even at the last, Man had given some thought to the future and had tried to preserve something for posterity.

That winter, the great waves of ice began their first assault on the mountains, attacking from north and south. The foothills were overwhelmed in the first onslaught, and the glaciers ground them into dust. But the mountains stood firm, and when the summer came the ice retreated for a while.

So, winter after winter, the battle continued, and the roar of the avalanches, the grinding of rock and the explosions of splintered ice filled the air with tumult. No war of Man's had been fiercer nor had engulfed the globe more completely than this. Until at last the tidal waves of ice began to subside and to creep slowly down the flanks of the mountains they had never quite subdued; though the valleys and passes were still firmly in their grip. It was stalemate: the glaciers had met their match.

But their defeat was too late to be of any use to Man.

So the centuries passed; and presently there happened something that must occur once at least in the history of every world in the Universe, no matter how remote and lonely it may be—

The ship from Venus came five thousand years too late, but its crew knew nothing of this. While still many millions of miles away, the telescopes had seen the great shroud of ice that made Earth the most brilliant object in the sky next to the Sun itself. Here and there the dazzling sheet was marred by black specks that revealed the presence of almost buried mountains. That was all. The rolling oceans, the plains and forests, the deserts and lakes – all that had been the world of Man was sealed beneath the ice, perhaps for ever.

The ship closed into Earth and established an orbit less than a thousand miles distant. For five days it circled the planet while cameras recorded all that was left to view and a hundred instruments gathered information that would give the Venusian scientists many years of work. An actual landing was not intended; there seemed little purpose in it. But on the sixth day the picture changed. A panoramic monitor, driven to the limit of its amplification, detected the dying radiation of the five-thousand-years-old beacon. Through all the centuries it had been sending out its signals, with ever-failing strength as its radioactive heart steadily weakened.

The monitor locked on the beacon frequency. In the control-room, a bell clamoured for attention. A little later, the Venusian ship broke free from its orbit and slanted down towards Earth – towards a range of mountains that still towered proudly above the ice, and to a cairn of grey stones that the years had scarcely touched.

The great disc of the Sun blazed fiercely in a sky no longer veiled with mist, for the clouds that had once hidden Venus had now completely gone. Whatever force had caused the change in the Sun's radiation had doomed one civilization but given birth to another. Less than five thousand years before, the half-savage people of Venus had seen Sun and stars for the first time. Just as the science of Earth had begun with astronomy, so had that of Venus, and on the warm, rich world that Man had never seen, progress had been incredibly rapid.

Perhaps the Venusians had been lucky. They never knew the Dark Age that held Man enchained for a thousand years; they missed the long detour into chemistry and mechanics, but came at once to the more fundamental laws of radiation physics. In the time that Man had taken to progress from the Pyramids to the rocket-propelled spaceship, the Venusians had passed from the discovery of agriculture to anti-gravity itself – the ultimate secret that Man had never learned.

The warm ocean that still bore most of the young planet's life rolled its breakers languidly against the sandy shore. So new was this continent that the very sands were coarse and gritty: there had not yet been time enough for the sea to wear them smooth. The scientists lay half in the water, their beautiful reptilian bodies gleaming in the sunlight. The greatest minds of Venus had gathered on this shore from all the islands of the planet. What they were going to hear they did not yet know, except that it concerned the Third World and the mysterious race that had peopled it before the coming of the ice.

The Historian was standing on the land, for the instruments he wished to use had no love of water. By his side was a large machine which attracted many curious glances from his colleagues. It was clearly concerned with optics, for a lens system projected from it towards a screen of white material a dozen yards away.

The Historian began to speak. Briefly he recapitulated what little had been discovered concerning the Third Planet and its people. He mentioned the centuries of fruitless research that had failed to interpret a single word of the writings of Earth. The planet had been inhabited by a race of great technical ability; that at least was proved by the few pieces of machinery that had been found in the cairn upon the mountain.

'We do not know why so advanced a civilization came to an end. Almost certainly, it had sufficient knowledge to survive an Ice Age. There must have been some other factor of which we know nothing. Possibly disease or racial degeneration may have been responsible. It has even been suggested that the tribal conflicts endemic to our own species in prehistoric times may have continued on the Third Planet after the coming of technology. Some philosophers maintain that knowledge of machinery does not necessarily imply a high degree of civilization, and it is theoretically possible to have wars in a society possessing mechanical power, flight, and even radio. Such a conception is very alien to our thoughts, but we must admit its possibility. It would certainly account for the downfall of the lost race.

'It has always been assumed that we should never know anything of the physical form of the creatures who lived on Planet Three. For centuries our artists have been depicting scenes from the history of the dead world, peopling it with all manner of fantastic beings. Most of these creations have resembled us more or less closely, though it has often been pointed out that because we are reptiles it does not follow that all intelligent life must necessarily be reptilian. We now know the answer to one of the most baffling problems of history. At last, after five hundred years of research, we have discovered the exact form and nature of the ruling life on the Third Planet.'

There was a murmur of astonishment from the assembled scientists. Some were so taken aback that they disappeared for a while into the comfort of the ocean, as all Venusians were apt to do in moments of stress. The Historian waited until his colleagues re-emerged into the element they so disliked. He himself was quite comfortable, thanks to tiny sprays that were continually playing over his body. With their help he could live on land for many hours before having to return to the ocean.

The excitement slowly subsided, and the lecturer continued.

'One of the most puzzling of the objects found on Planet Three was a flat metal container holding a great length of transparent plastic material, perforated at the edges and wound tightly into a spool. This transparent tape at first seemed quite featureless, but an examination with the new sub-electronic microscope has shown that this is not the case. Along the surface of the material, invisible to our eyes but perfectly clear under the correct radiation, are literally thousands of tiny pictures. It is believed that they were imprinted on the material by some chemical means, and have faded with the passage of time.

'These pictures apparently form a record of life as it was on the Third Planet at the height of its civilization. They are not independent; consecutive pictures are almost identical, differing only in the detail of movement. The purpose of such a record is obvious: it is only necessary to project the scenes in rapid succession to give an illusion of continuous movement. We have made a machine to do this, and I have here an exact reproduction of the picture sequence.

'The scenes you are now going to witness take us back many

thousands of years to the great days of our sister planet. They show a very complex civilization, many of whose activities we can only dimly understand. Life seems to have been very violent and energetic, and much that you will see is quite baffling.

'It is clear that the Third Planet was inhabited by a number of different species, none of them reptilian. That is a blow to our pride, but the conclusion is inescapable. The dominant type of life appears to have been a two-armed biped. It walked upright and covered its body with some flexible material, possibly for protection against the cold, since even before the Ice Age the planet was at a much lower temperature than our own world.

'But I will not try your patience any further. You will now see the record of which I have been speaking.'

A brilliant light flashed from the projector. There was a gentle whirring, and on the screen appeared hundreds of strange beings moving rather jerkily to and fro. The picture expanded to embrace one of the creatures, and the scientists could see that the Historian's description had been correct. The creature possessed two eyes, set rather closely together, but the other facial adornments were a little obscure. There was a large orifice in the lower portion of the head that was continually opening and closing; possibly it had something to do with the creature's breathing.

The scientists watched spellbound as the strange beings became involved in a series of fantastic adventures. There was an incredibly violent conflict with another, slightly different, creature. It seemed certain that they must both be killed – but no; when it was all over neither seemed any the worse. Then came a furious drive over miles of country in a four-wheeled mechanical device which was capable of extraordinary feats of locomotion. The ride ended in a city packed with other vehicles moving in all directions at breath-taking speeds. No one was surprised to see two of the machines meet head-on, with devastating results.

After that, events became even more complicated. It was now quite obvious that it would take many years of research to analyse and understand all that was happening. It was also clear that the record was a work of art, somewhat stylized, rather than an exact reproduction of life as it actually had been on the Third Planet.

Most of the scientists felt themselves completely dazed when the sequence of pictures came to an end. There was a final flurry of motion, in which the creature that had been the centre of interest became involved in some tremendous but incomprehensible catastrophe. The picture contracted to a circle, centred on the creature's head. The last scene of all was an expanded view of its face, obviously expressing some powerful emotion, but whether it was rage, grief, defiance, resignation or some other feeling could not be guessed.

The picture vanished. For a moment some lettering appeared on the screen; then it was all over.

For several minutes there was complete silence, save for the lapping of the waves on the sand. The scientists were too stunned to speak. The fleeting glimpse of Earth's civilization had had a shattering effect on their minds. Then little groups began to start talking together, first in whispers and then more loudly as the implications of what they had seen became clearer. Presently the Historian called for attention and addressed the meeting again.

'We are now planning,' he began, 'a vast programme of research to extract all available knowledge from the record. Thousands of copies are being made for distribution to all workers. You will appreciate the problems involved; the psychologists in particular have an immense task confronting them. But I do not doubt that we shall succeed. In another generation, who can say what we may not have learned of this wonderful race? Before we leave, let us look again at our remote cousins, whose wisdom may have surpassed our own but of whom so little has survived.'

Once more the final picture flashed on the screen, motionless this time, for the projector had been stopped. With something like awe, the scientists gazed at the still figure from the past, while in turn the little biped stared back at them with its characteristic expression of arrogant bad temper.

For the rest of Time it would symbolize the human race. The psychologists of Venus would analyse its actions and watch its every movement until they could reconstruct its mind. Thousands of books would be written about it. Intricate philosophies would be contrived to account for its behaviour. But all this labour, all this research, would be utterly in vain.

Perhaps the proud and lonely figure on the screen was smiling sardonically at the scientists who were starting on their age-long, fruitless quest. Its secret would be safe as long as the Universe endured, for no one now would ever read the lost language of Earth. Millions of times in the ages to come those last few words would flash across the screen, and none could ever guess their meaning:

A Walt Disney Production.

The Sentinel

ARTHUR C. CLARKE

The Sentinel *is the second story written by Arthur C. Clarke included in this anthology. It was written at Christmas in 1948 and has subsequently played an important part in popular science fiction, as it formed the basis of* 2001 : a Space Odyssey.

Although The Sentinel *was printed in* The Avon Science Fiction and Fantasy Reader (1951) *three years before* Expedition to Earth *was first published, it has in it some features which are inverted in the later story. For example, life on the Moon died at the moment that it began on Earth, just as life on Earth died just as it began on Venus. Both calamities occurred because of natural disasters which could not be controlled by intelligent beings.* The Sentinel, *however, turns the reader relentlessly towards the future and its last sentence ominously (or hopefully?) looks for an alien invasion of our planet very soon.*

The story is full of surprises, although the opening is deliberately low-keyed. Even exploration of the Moon can become dull: 'There is nothing hazardous or even particularly exciting about lunar exploration.' The lunar travellers cook bacon and sausages for breakfast before they notice a metallic glint on the top of a distant mountain. All good short stories, whether they are science fiction or not, must have what Aristotle would have called 'peripates' – turning points which mark a change from one state of things to another, perhaps opposite, state of things, from placidness to excitement, from dull routine to unexpected challenge. It is from such 'peripates' that much of the drama in The Sentinel *springs, but to use such devices with effect demands a high degree of skill in composition.*

This skill of Arthur C. Clarke was noticed in the introduction to Expedition to Earth *and once more, here in* The Sentinel, *we notice his use of description of the landscape and the universe to reflect the prevalent mood of his action. There is, moreover, a lyricism in his writing which evokes the spaciousness and the mystery of the creation he is describing:*

'Such was our own Earth, the smoke of the great volcanoes still staining the skies, when that first ship of the peoples of the dawn came sliding in from the abyss beyond Pluto. It passed the frozen outer worlds, knowing that life could play no part in their destinies. It came to rest among the inner planets, warming themselves around the fire of the Sun and waiting for their stories to begin.'

There is, too, in The Sentinel *the same trace of Clarke's humour which runs through the seriousness of his stories. As the astronaut seeks for answers to his questions and looks at the Pyramid he imagines it replying, 'Sorry, I'm a stranger here myself.' But our own researches carry with them their own warning: 'we have broken the glass of the fire-alarm and have nothing to do but wait' – except, perhaps, to prove our fitness as a race to survive?*

The next time you see the full Moon high in the south, look carefully at its right-hand edge and let your eye travel upwards along the curve of the disc. Round about two o'clock, you will notice a small, dark oval: anyone with normal eyesight can find it quite easily. It is the great walled plain, one of the finest on the Moon, known as the Mare Crisium – the Sea of Crises. Three hundred miles in diameter – and almost completely surrounded by a ring of magnificent mountains, it had never been explored until we entered it in the late summer of 1966.

Our expedition was a large one. We had two heavy freighters which had flown our supplies and equipment from the main lunar base in the Mare Serenitatis, five hundred miles away. There were also three small rockets which were intended for short-range transport over regions which our surface vehicles could not cross. Luckily, most of the Mare Crisium is very flat. There are none of the great crevasses so common and so dangerous elsewhere, and very few craters or mountains of any size. As far as we could tell, our powerful caterpillar tractors would have no difficulty in taking us wherever we wished.

I was geologist – or selenologist, if you want to be pedantic – in charge of the group exploring the southern region of the Mare. We had crossed a hundred miles of it in a week, skirting the foothills of the mountains along the shore of what was once the ancient sea, some thousand million years before. When life was beginning on Earth, it was already dying here. The waters were retreating down the flanks of those stupendous cliffs, retreating into the empty heart of the Moon. Over the land which we were crossing, the tideless ocean had once been half a mile deep and now the only trace of moisture was the hoar frost one could sometimes find in caves which the searing sunlight never penetrated.

We had begun our journey early in the slow lunar dawn, and still had almost a week of Earth-time before nightfall. Half a dozen times a day we would leave our vehicle and go outside in the space-suits to hunt for interesting minerals, or to place markers for the guidance of future travellers. It was an uneventful routine. There is nothing hazardous or even particularly exciting about lunar exploration. We could live comfortably for a month in our pressurized tractors, and if we ran into trouble we could always radio for help and sit tight until one of the spaceships came to our rescue. When that happened there was always a frightful outcry about the waste of rocket fuel, so a tractor sent out an SOS only in a real emergency.

I said just now that there was nothing exciting about lunar exploration, but of course that is not true. One could never grow tired of those incredible mountains, so much more rugged than the gentle hills of Earth. We never knew, as we rounded the capes and promontories of that vanished sea, what new splendours would be revealed to us. The whole southern curve of the Mare Crisium is a vast delta where a score of rivers had once found their way into the ocean, fed perhaps by the torrential rains that must have lashed the mountains in the brief volcanic age when the moon was young. Each of these ancient valleys was an invitation, challenging us to climb into the unknown uplands beyond. But we had a hundred miles still to cover, and could only look longingly at the heights which others must scale.

We kept Earth-time aboard the tractor, and precisely at 22.00 hours the final radio message would be sent out to base and we could close down for the day. Outside, the rocks would still be burning beneath the almost vertical sun, but to us it was night until we awoke again eight hours later. Then one of us would prepare breakfast, there would be a great buzzing of electric shavers and someone would switch on the short-wave radio from Earth. Indeed, when the smell of frying bacon began to fill the cabin, it was sometimes hard to believe that we were not back on our own world – everything was so normal and homely, apart from the feeling of decreased weight and the unnatural slowness with which objects fell.

It was my turn to prepare breakfast in the corner of the main cabin that served as a galley. I can remember that moment quite vividly after all these years, for the radio had just played one of my favourite melodies, the old Welsh air, 'David of the White Rock'. Our driver was already outside in his space-suit, inspecting our caterpillar treads. My assistant, Louis Garnett, was up forward in the control position, making some belated entries in yesterday's log.

As I stood by the frying-pan, waiting, like any terrestrial housewife, for the sausages to brown, I let my gaze wander idly over the mountain walls which covered the whole of the southern horizon, marching out of sight to the east and west below the curve of the Moon. They seemed only a mile or two from the tractor, but I knew that the nearest was twenty miles away. On the Moon, of course, there is no loss of detail with distance – none of that almost imperceptible haziness which softens and sometimes transfigures all far-off things on Earth.

Those mountains were ten thousand feet high, and they climbed steeply out of the plain as if ages ago some subterranean eruption had smashed them skywards through the molten crust. The base of even the nearest was hidden from sight by the steeply curving surface of the plain, for the Moon is a very little world, and from where I was standing the horizon was only two miles away.

I lifted my eyes towards the peaks which no man had ever climbed, the peaks which, before the coming of terrestrial life, had watched the retreating oceans sink sullenly into their graves, taking with them the hope and morning promise of a world. The sunlight was beating against those ramparts with a glare that hurt the eyes, yet only a little way above them the stars were shining steadily in a sky blacker than a winter midnight on Earth.

I was turning away when my eye caught a metallic glitter high on the ridge of a great promontory thrusting out into the sea thirty miles to the west. It was a dimensionless point of light as if a star had been clawed from the sky by one of those cruel peaks, and I imagined that some smooth rock-surface was catching the sunlight and heliographing it straight into my eyes. Such things were not uncommon. When the Moon is in her second quarter, observers on Earth can sometimes see the great ranges in the Oceanus Procellarum burning with a blue-white iridescence as the sunlight flashes from their slopes and leaps again from world to world. But I was curious to know what kind of rock could be shining so brightly up there, and I climbed into the observation turret and swung our four-inch telescope round to the west.

I could see just enough to tantalize me. Clear and sharp in the field of vision, the mountain peaks seemed only half a mile away, but whatever was catching the sunlight was still too small to be resolved. Yet it seemed to have an elusive symmetry, and the summit upon which it rested was curiously flat. I stared for a long time at that glittering enigma, straining my eyes into space, until presently a smell of burning from the galley told me that our breakfast sausages had made their quarter-million-mile journey in vain.

All that morning we argued our way across the Mare Crisium while the western mountains reared higher in the sky. Even when we were out prospecting in the space-suits, the discussion would continue over the radio. It was absolutely certain, my companions argued, that there had never been any form of intelligent life on the Moon. The only living things that had ever existed there were a few primitive plants and their slightly less degenerate ancestors. I knew that as well as anyone, but there are times when a scientist must not be afraid to make a fool of himself.

'Listen,' I said at last, 'I'm going up there, if only for my own peace of mind. That mountain's less than twelve thousand feet high – that's only two thousand under Earth gravity – and I can make the trip in twenty hours at the outside. I've always wanted to go up into those hills, anyway, and this gives me an excellent excuse.'

'If you don't break your neck,' said Garnett, 'you'll be the laughing-stock of the expedition when we get back to base. That mountain will probably be called Wilson's Folly from now on.'

'I won't break my neck,' I said firmly. 'Who was the first man to climb Pico and Helicon?'

'But weren't you rather younger in those days?' asked Louis gently.

'That,' I said with great dignity, 'is as good a reason as any for going.'

We went to bed early that night, after driving the tractor to within half a mile of the promontory. Garnett was coming with me in the morning; he was a good climber, and had often been with me on such exploits before. Our driver was only too glad to be left in charge of the machine.

At first sight, those cliffs seemed completely unscalable, but to anyone with a good head for heights, climbing is easy on a world where all weights are only a sixth of their normal value. The real danger in lunar mountaineering lies in over-confidence; a six-hundred-foot drop on the Moon can kill you just as thoroughly as a hundred-foot fall on Earth.

We made our first halt on a wide ledge about four thousand feet above the plain. Climbing had not been very difficult but my limbs were stiff with the unaccustomed effort, and I was glad of the rest. We could still see the tractor as a tiny metal insect far down at the foot of the cliff, and we reported our progress to the driver before starting on the next ascent.

Hour by hour the horizon widened and more and more of the great plain came into sight. Now we could look for fifty miles out across the Mare, and even see the peaks of the mountains on the opposite coast more than a hundred miles away. Few of the great lunar plains are as smooth as the Mare Crisium, and we could almost imagine that a sea of water and not of rock was lying there two miles below. Only a group of crater pits low down on the skyline spoiled the illusion.

Our goal was still invisible over the crest of the mountain and we were steering by maps, using the Earth as a guide. Almost due east of us, that great silver crescent hung low over the plain, already well into its first quarter. The Sun and the stars would make their slow march across the sky and would sink presently from sight, but Earth would always be there, never moving from her appointed place, waxing and waning as the years and seasons passed. In ten days' time she would be a blinding disc bathing these rocks with her midnight radiance, fifty-fold brighter than the full moon. But we must be out of the mountains long before night, or else we would remain among them for ever.

Inside our suits it was comfortably cool, for the refrigeration units were fighting the fierce Sun and carrying away the body-heat of our exertions. We seldom spoke to each other, except to pass climbing instructions and to discuss our best plan of ascent. I do not know what Garnett was thinking, probably that this was the craziest goose chase he had ever embarked upon. I more than half agreed with him, but the joy of climbing, the knowledge that no man had ever gone this way before and the exhilaration of the steadily widening landscape gave me all the reward I needed.

I do not think I was particularly excited when I saw in front of us the wall of rock I had first inspected through the telescope from thirty miles away. It would level off about fifty feet above our heads, and there on the plateau would be the thing that had lured me over these barren wastes. It was, almost certainly, nothing more than a boulder splintered ages ago by a falling meteor, and with its cleavage planes still fresh and bright in this incorruptible, unchanging silence.

There were no hand-holds on the rock face and we had to use a grapnel. My tired arms seemed to gain new strength as I swung the three-pronged metal anchor round my head and sent it sailing up towards the stars. The first time it broke loose and came falling slowly back when we pulled the rope. On the third attempt, the prongs gripped firmly and our combined weights could not shift it.

Garnett looked at me anxiously. I could tell that he wanted to go first, but I smiled back at him through the glass of my helmet and shook my head. Slowly, taking my time, I began the final ascent.

Even with my space-suit, I only weighed forty pounds here, so I pulled myself up hand over hand without bothering to use my feet. At the rim I paused and waved to my companion, then I scrambled over the edge and stood upright, staring ahead of me.

You must understand that until this very moment I had been almost completely convinced that there could be nothing strange or unusual for me to find here. Almost, but not quite; it was that haunting doubt that had driven me forwards. Well, it was a doubt no longer, but the haunting had scarcely begun.

I was standing on a plateau perhaps a hundred feet across. It had once been smooth – too smooth to be natural – but falling meteors had pitted and scored its surface through immeasurable aeons. It had been levelled to support a glittering roughly pyramidal structure, twice as high as a man, that was set in the rock like a gigantic, many-faceted jewel.

Probably no emotion at all filled my mind in those first few seconds. Then I felt a great lifting of my heart, and a strange inexpressible joy. For I loved the Moon, and now I knew that the creeping moss of Aristarchus and Eratosthenes was not the only life she had brought forth in her youth. The old, discredited dream of the first explorers was true. There had, after all, been a lunar civilization – and I was the first to find it. That I had come perhaps a hundred million years too late did not distress me; it was enough to have come at all.

My mind was beginning to function normally, to analyse and to ask questions. Was this a building, a shrine – or something for which my language had no name? If a building, then why was it erected in so uniquely inaccessible a spot? I wondered if it might be a temple, and I could picture the adepts of some strange priesthood calling on their gods to preserve them as the life of the Moon ebbed with the dying oceans, and calling on their gods in vain.

I took a dozen steps forward to examine the thing more closely, but some sense of caution kept me from going too near. I knew a little of archaeology, and tried to guess the cultural level of the civilization that must have smoothed this mountain and raised the glittering mirror surfaces that still dazzled my eyes.

The Egyptians could have done it, I thought, if their workmen had possessed whatever strange materials these far more ancient architects had used. Because of the thing's smallness, it did not occur to me that I might be looking at the handiwork of a race more advanced than my own. The idea that the Moon had possessed intelligence at all was still almost too tremendous to grasp, and my pride would not let me take the final, humiliating plunge.

And then I noticed something that set the scalp crawling at the back of my neck – something so trivial and so innocent that many would never have noticed it at all. I have said that the plateau was scarred by meteors; it was also coated inches deep with the cosmic dust that is always filtering down upon the surface of any world where there are no winds to disturb it. Yet the dust and the meteor scratches ended quite abruptly in a wide circle enclosing the little pyramid, as though an invisible wall was protecting it from the ravages of time and the slow but ceaseless bombardment from space.

There was someone shouting in my earphones, and I realized that Garnett had been calling me for some time. I walked unsteadily to the edge of the cliff and signalled him to join me, not trusting myself to speak. Then I went back towards that circle in the dust. I picked up a fragment of splintered rock and tossed it gently towards the shining enigma. If the pebble had vanished at that invisible barrier I should not have been surprised, but it seemed to hit a smooth, hemispherical surface and slide gently to the ground.

I knew then that I was looking at nothing that could be matched in the antiquity of my own race. This was not a building, but a machine, protecting itself with forces that had challenged Eternity. Those forces, whatever they might be, were still operating, and perhaps I had already come too close. I thought of all the radiations man had trapped and tamed in the past century. For all I knew, I might be as irrevocably doomed as if I had stepped into the deadly, silent aura of an unshielded atomic pile.

I remember turning then towards Garnett, who had joined me and was now standing motionless at my side. He seemed quite oblivious of me, so I did not disturb him but walked to the edge of the cliff in an effort to marshal my thoughts. There below me lay the Mare Crisium – Sea of Crises, indeed – strange and weird to most men, but reassuringly familiar to me. I lifted my eyes towards the crescent Earth, lying in her cradle of stars, and I wondered what her clouds had covered when these unknown builders had finished their work. Was it the steaming jungle of the Carboniferous, the bleak shoreline over which the first amphibians must crawl to conquer the land – or, earlier still, the long loneliness before the coming of life?

Do not ask me why I did not guess the truth sooner – the truth that seems so obvious now. In the first excitement of my discovery, I had assumed without question that this crystalline apparition had been built by some race belonging to the Moon's remote past, but suddenly, and with overwhelming force, the belief came to me that it was as alien to the Moon as I myself.

In twenty years we had found no trace of life but a few degenerate plants. No lunar civilization, whatever its doom, could have left but a single token of its existence.

I looked at the shining pyramid again, and the more remote it seemed from anything that had to do with the Moon. And suddenly I felt myself shaking with a foolish, hysterical laughter, brought on by excitement and over-exertion: for I imagined that the little pyramid was speaking to me and was saying: 'Sorry, I'm a stranger here myself.'

It has taken us twenty years to crack that invisible shield and to reach the machine inside those crystal walls. What we could not understand, we broke at last with the savage might of atomic power and now I have seen the fragments of the lovely, glittering thing I found up there on the mountain.

They are meaningless. The mechanisms – if indeed they are mechanisms – of the pyramid belong to a technology that lies far beyond our horizon, perhaps to the technology of paraphysical forces.

The mystery haunts us all the more now that the other planets have been reached and we know that only Earth has ever been the home of intelligent life. Nor could any lost civilization of our own world have built that machine, for the thickness of the meteoric dust on the plateau has enabled us to measure its age. It was set there upon its mountain before life had emerged from the seas of Earth.

When our world was half its present age, *something* from the stars swept through the Solar System, left this token of its passage, and went again upon its way. Until we destroyed it, that machine was still fulfilling the purpose of its builders; and as to that purpose, here is my guess.

Nearly a hundred thousand million stars are turning in the circle of the Milky Way, and long ago other races on the worlds of other suns must have scaled and passed the heights that we have reached. Think of such civilizations, far back in time against the fading after-glow of Creation, masters of a universe so young that life as yet had come only to a handful of worlds. Theirs would have been a loneliness we cannot imagine, the loneliness of gods looking out across infinity and finding none to share their thoughts.

They must have searched the star-clusters as we have searched the planets. Everywhere there would be worlds, but they would be empty or peopled with crawling, mindless things. Such was our own Earth, the smoke of the great volcanoes still staining the skies, when that first ship of the peoples of the dawn came sliding in from the abyss beyond Pluto. It passed the frozen outer worlds, knowing that life could play no part in their destinies. It came to rest among the inner planets, warming themselves around the fire of the Sun and waiting for their stories to begin.

Those wanderers must have looked on Earth, circling safely in the narrow zone between fire and ice, and must have guessed that it was the favourite of the Sun's children. Here, in the distant future, would be intelligence; but there were countless stars before them still, and they might never come this way again.

So they left a sentinel, one of millions they have scattered throughout the universe, watching over all worlds with the promise of life. It was a beacon that down the ages has been patiently signalling the fact that no one had discovered it.

Perhaps you understand now why that crystal pyramid was set upon the Moon instead of on the Earth. Its builders were not concerned with races still struggling up from savagery. They would be interested in our civilization only if we proved our fitness to survive – by crossing space and so escaping from the Earth, our cradle. That is the challenge that all intelligent races must meet, sooner or later. It is a double challenge, for it depends in turn upon the conquest of atomic energy and the last choice between life and death.

Once we had passed that crisis, it was only a matter of time before we found the pyramid and forced it open. Now its signals have ceased, and those whose duty it is will be turning their minds upon Earth. Perhaps they wish to help our infant civilization. But they must be very, very old, and the old are often insanely jealous of the young.

I can never look now at the Milky Way without wondering from which of those banked clouds of stars the emissaries are coming. If you will pardon so commonplace a simile, we have broken the glass of the fire-alarm and have nothing to do but to wait.

I do not think we will have to wait for long.

The Inheritors

WILLIAM GOLDING

William Golding published The Inheritors *in 1955 and it quickly won critical acclaim. It poses real difficulties for the reader, however, many of which spring from the fact that the author puts the reader in the position of his heroes, the Neanderthalers; their bewilderment at the men they meet is reflected in the accounts of what they see, of what they say, and in the conclusions they draw from what they see and say.The reader experiences the difficulties of the Neanderthalers for himself.*

In The Lord of the Flies *Golding inverted the world of R. M. Ballantyne's* Coral Island *and in* The Inheritors *he inverts the world of H. G. Wells's short story* The Grisly Folk, *where Wells's Neanderthalers are very much the same sort of creatures he described in his* Outline of History *(quoted by Golding at the front of his novel):*

> *'We know very little of the appearance of the Neanderthal man, but this . . . seems to suggest an extreme hairiness, an ugliness, or a repulsive strangeness in his appearance over and above his low forehead, his beetle brows, his ape neck, and his inferior stature. . . . The dim racial remembrance of such gorilla-like monsters, with cunning brains, shambling gait, hairy bodies, strong teeth, and possibly cannibalistic tendencies, may be the germ of the ogre in folklore.'*

It is interesting to compare this description with the Neanderthalers' own description of man in this extract. In Golding's novel they are the inverse of Wells's; they reveal a great pathos in their failure to understand man: innocence, honesty and simplicity come into contact with the fearful, aggressive, tribalism of mankind.

In the following passage Fa and Lok witness a strange, superstitious and horrifying ritual as the men, half-starved and terrified, seek ways to appease the forces against them. The screen of bushes, the Stag, the incantation, the witch-doctor's dance, and the 'sacrifice' of Pine-tree's finger all play a part in the ritual, the significance of which the Neanderthalers just cannot understand. Their bewilder-

ment is seen in the manner of the account, their language and their behaviour. The style of Golding reflects their predicament and emphasizes his implicit social comment about Man's presumed superiority and greater sophistication.

Fa pushed him to one side. They stood up together and looked round the overhang. The bleak air of first dawn poured round them. Fa went into a recess and came back with an almost meatless bone and some scraps that the hyenas had not been able to reach. The people were red again, copper red and sandy for the blue and grey of the night had left them. They said nothing but picked away and shared the scraps with a passion of pity for each other. Presently they wiped their hands on their thighs and went down to the water and drank. Then still without speaking or sharing a picture they turned to the left and went to the corner round which lay the cliff.

Fa stopped.

'I do not want to see.'

Together they turned and looked at the empty overhang.

'I will take the fire when it falls from the sky or wakes among the heather.'

Lok considered the picture of fire. Otherwise there was an emptiness in his head and only the tidal feeling, deep and sure, was noticeable inside him. He began to walk towards the logs at the other end of the terrace. Fa caught him by the wrist.

'We shall not go again on the island.'

Lok faced her, his hands up.

'There must be food found for Liku. So that she will be strong when she comes back.'

Fa looked deeply at him and there were things in her face that he could not understand. He took a step sideways, shrugged, gesticulated. He stopped and waited anxiously.

'No!'

She held him by the wrist and lugged him. He resisted, talking all the time. He did not know what he said. She stopped pulling and faced him again.

'You will be killed.'

There was a pause. Lok looked at her, then at the island. He scratched his left cheek. Fa came close.

'I shall have children that do not die in the cave by the sea. There will be a fire.'

'Liku will have children when she is a woman.'

She let go of his wrist again.

'Listen. Do not speak. The new people took the log and Mal died. Ha was on the cliff and a new man was on the cliff. Ha died. The new people came to the overhang. Nil and the old woman died.'

The light was much stronger behind her. There was a fleck of red in the sky over her head. She grew in his sight. She was the woman. Lok shook his head at her humbly. Her words had made the feeling rise.

'When the new people bring Liku back I shall be glad.'

Fa made a high, angry sound, she took a step to the water and came back again. She grabbed him by his shoulders.

'How can they give the new one milk? Does a stag give milk? And what if they do not bring back Liku?'

He answered humbly out of an empty head.

'I do not see this picture.'

She left him in her anger, turned away and stood with a hand on the corner where the cliff began. He could see how she was bristling and how the muscles of her shoulder twitched. She was bent, leaning forward, right hand on right knee. He heard her mutter at him with her back still turned.

'You have fewer pictures than the new one.'

Lok put the heels of his hands in his eyes and pressed so that spokes of light flashed in them like the river.

'There has not been a night.'

That was real. Where the night should have been was a greyness. Not only his ears and his nose had been awake after they had lain together, but the Lok inside them, watching the feeling rise and ebb and rise. There was stuffed inside the bones of his head the white flock of the autumn creepers, their seeds were in his nose, making him yawn and sneeze. He put his hands apart and blinked at where Fa had been. Now she was backed on this side of the rock and peering round it at the river. Her hand beckoned.

The log was out again. It was near the island and the same two bone-faces were sitting at either end. They were digging the water and the log was sidling across the river. When it was near the bank and the swarming bushes it straightened into the current and the men stopped digging. They were looking closely at the clear patch by the water where the dead tree was. Lok could see how one turned and spoke to the other.

Fa touched his hand.

'They are looking for something.'

The log drifted gently downstream with the current and the sun was rising. The farther reaches of the river burst into flame, so that for a time the forest on either side was dark by contrast. The indefinable attraction of the new people pushed the flock out of Lok's head. He forgot to blink.

The log was smaller, drifting down away from the fall. When it turned askew, the man in the back would dig again and the log would point straight at Lok's eyes. Always, the two men looked sideways at the bank.

Fa muttered:

'There is another log.'

The bushes by the island shore were shaking busily. They parted for a moment and now that he knew where to look Lok could see the end of another log hidden close in. A man thrust his head and shoulders through the green leaves and waved an arm angrily. The two men in the log began to dig quickly until it had moved right up to where the man waved opposite the dead tree. Now they were no longer looking at the dead tree but at the man, and nodding their heads at him. The log brought them to him and nosed under the bushes.

Curiosity overcame Lok; he began to run towards the new way on to the island so excitedly that Fa shared his picture. She got him again, and grabbed him.

'No! No!'

Lok jabbered. Fa shouted at him.

'I say "No!"'

She pointed at the overhang.

'What did you say? Fa has many pictures—'

At last he was silent and waiting for her. She spoke solemnly.

'We shall go down into the forest. For food. We shall watch them across the river.'

They ran down the slope away from the river, keeping the rocks between them and the new people. In the skirts of the forest there was food; bulbs that just showed a point of green, grubs and shoots, fungi, the tender inside of some kinds of bark. The meat of the doe was still in them and they were not hungry as the people counted hunger. They could eat, where there was food; but without it they could go for to-day easily and for to-morrow if they had to. For this reason there was no urgency in their searching so that presently the enchantment of the new people drew them again to the bushes at the edge of the water. They stood, toes gripped in the mire, and listened for the new people through the noise of the fall. An early fly buzzed at Lok's nose. The air was warm and the sun softly bright so that he yawned again. Then he heard the new people making their bird-noises of conversation and a number of other unexplained sounds, bumps and creakings. Fa sneaked to the edge of the clearing by the dead tree and lay on the earth.

There was nothing to be seen across the water, yet the bumps and creaks continued.

'Fa. Climb the dead trunk to see.'

She turned her face and looked at him doubtfully. All at once he realized that she was going to say no, was going to insist that they went away from the new people and put a great gap of time between them and Liku; and this became a knowledge that was unbearable. He sneaked quickly forward on all fours and ran up the concealed side of the dead tree. In a moment he was burrowing through the shock-head among the dusty, dark, sour-smelling ivy leaves. He had hardly lifted his last limb into the hollow top before Fa's head broke through behind him.

The top of the tree was empty like a great acorn cup. It was white, soft wood that gave and moulded to their weight and was full of food. The ivy spread upwards and downwards in a dark tangle so that they might have been sitting in a bush on the ground. The other trees overtopped them but there was open sky towards the river and the green drifts of the island. Parting the leaves cautiously as if he were looking for eggs, Lok found that he could make a hole no bigger than the eye-part of his face; and though the edges of the hole moved a little he could see the river and the other banks, all the brighter for the dark green leaves round the hole – as though he had cupped his hands and was looking through them. On his left Fa was making herself a lookout, and the edge of the cup even gave her something to rest her elbows on. The heavy feeling sank in Lok as it always did when he had the new people to watch. He sagged luxuriously. Then suddenly they forgot everything else and were very still.

The log was sliding out of the bushes by the island. The two men were digging carefully and the log was turning. It did not point at Lok and Fa but upstream, though it began to move across river towards them. There were many new things in the hollow of the log; shapes like rocks and bulging skins. There were all kinds of sticks, from long poles without leaves or branches to sprays of withering green. The log came close.

At last they saw the new people face to face and in sunlight. They were incomprehensibly strange. Their hair was black and grew in the most unexpected ways. The bone-face in the front of the log had a pine-tree of hair that stood straight up so that his head, already too long, was drawn out as though something were pulling it upward without mercy. The other bone-face had hair in a huge bush that stood out on all sides like the ivy on the dead tree.

There was hair growing thickly over their bodies about the waist, the belly and the upper part of the leg so that this part of them was thicker than the rest. Yet Lok did not look immediately at their bodies; he was far too absorbed in the stuff around their eyes. A piece of white bone was placed under them, fitting close, and where the broad nostrils should have shown were narrow slits and between them the bone was drawn out to a point. Under that was another slit over the mouth, and their voices came fluttering through it. There was a little dark hair jutting out under the slit. The eyes of the face that peered through all this bone were dark and busy. There were eyebrows above them, thinner than the mouth or the nostrils, black, curving out and up so that the men looked menacing and wasp-like. Lines of teeth and seashells hung round their necks, over grey, furry skin. Over the eyebrows the bone bulged up and swept back to be hidden under the hair. As the log came closer, Lok could see that the colour was not really bone white and shining but duller. It was more the colour of the big fungi, the ears that the people ate, and something like them in texture. Their legs and arms were stick-thin so that the joints were like the nodes in a twig.

Now that Lok was looking almost into the log he saw that it was much broader than before; or rather that it was the two logs moving side by side. There were more bundles and curious shapes in this log and a man lay among them on his side. His body and bone was like the others but his hair grew on his head in a mass of sharp points that glistened and looked hard as the points on a chestnut case. He was doing something to one of the sharp twigs and his curved stick lay beside him.

The logs sidled right into the bank. The man at the back – Lok thought of him as Pine-tree – spoke softly. Bush laid down his wooden leaf and caught hold of the grass of the bank. Chestnut-head took his curved stick and twig and stole across the logs until he was crouched on the earth itself. Lok and Fa were almost directly above him. They could smell his individual scent, a sea-smell, meat-smell, fearsome and exciting. He was so close that any moment he might wind them for all he was below them and Lok inhibited his own scent in sudden fear, though he did not know what he did. He reduced his breathing till it was the merest surface and the very leaves were more lively.

Chestnut-head stood under them in the sun pattern. The twig was across the curved stick. He looked this way and that round the dead tree, he inspected the ground, he looked forward again into the forest. He spoke sideways to the others in the boat out of his slit; soft twittering speech; the whiteness quivered.

Lok felt the shock of a man who has trusted to a bough that is not there. He understood in a kind of upside-down sensation that there was no Mal face, Fa face, Lok face concealed under the bone. It was skin.

Bush and Pine-tree had done something with strips of hide that joined the logs to the bushes. They got quickly out of the log and ran forward out of sight. Presently there was the sound of someone striking stone against wood. Chestnut-head crept forward too and was hidden.

There was nothing of interest now but the logs. They were very smooth and shiny inside where the wood could be seen and outside there were long smears like the whiteness on a rock when the sea has gone back and the sun has dried it. The edges were rounded, depressed in places where the hands of the bone-faces had rested. The shapes inside them were too various and numerous to be sorted. There were round stones, sticks, hides, there were bundles bigger than Lok, there were patterns of vivid red, bones that had grown into live shapes, the very ends of the brown leaves where the men held them were shaped like brown fish, there were smells, there were questions and no answers. Lok looked without seeing and the picture slid apart and came together again. Across the water there was no movement on the island.

Fa touched him on the hand. She was turning herself in the tree. Lok followed her carefully and they made themselves spy-holes that looked down into the clearing.

Already the familiar had altered. The tangle of bush and stagnant water to the left of the clearing was the same and so was the impenetrable marsh to the right. But where the trail through the forest touched the clearing thorn bushes were now growing thickly. There was a gap in these bushes and as they watched they saw Pine-tree come through the gap with another thorn bush over his shoulder. The stem was clean white and pointed. In the forest behind him the noise of chopping went on.

Fear was coming from Fa. It was not a shared picture but a general sense, a bitter smell, a dead silence and agonized attention, a motionlessness and tensed awareness that began to call forth the same in him. Now, more clearly than ever before there were two Loks, outside and inside. The inner Lok could look for ever. But the outer that breathed and heard and smelt and was awake always, was insistent and tightening on him like another skin. It forced the knowledge of its fear, its sense of peril on him long before his brain could understand the picture. He was more frightened than ever before in his life, more than when he had crouched on a rock with Ha and a cat had paced to and fro by a drained kill, looking up and wondering whether they were worth the trouble.

Fa's mouth crept to his ear.

'We are shut in.'

The thorn bushes spread. They were very thick where there was an easy way into the clearing; but there were others now, two lines of them by the stagnant water and by the marsh. The clearing was a half-ring open only to the water of the river. The three bone-faces came through the last gap, with more thorn bushes. With these they closed the way behind them.

Fa whispered in his ear.

'They know we are here. They do not want us to go away.'

All the same the bone-faces ignored them. Bush and Pine-tree went back and the logs bumped each other. Chestnut-head began to pace slowly round the line of thorn bushes, keeping his face to the forest. Always the bent stick was held with a twig across it. The thorn bushes were up to his chest and when a bull bellowed far off on the plains he froze, face lifted and the stick unbent a little. The woodpigeons were talking again and the sun looked down into the top of the dead tree and breathed warmly on the two people.

Someone dug noisily in the water and the logs bumped. There were wooden knockings, draggings and bird speech; then two other men came from under the tree into the clearing. The first man was like the others. His hair gathered into a tuft on top of his head then spread so that it bobbed as he moved. Tuft went straight to the thorn bushes and began to watch the forest. He also had a bent stick and a twig.

The second man was unlike the others. He was broader and shorter. There was much hair on his body and his head-hair was sleek as if fat had been rubbed in it. The hair lay in a ball at the back of his neck. He had no hair on the front of his head at all so that the sweep of bone skin, daunting in its fungoid pallor, came right over above his ears. Now for the first time, Lok saw the ears of the new men. They were tiny and screwed tightly into the sides of their heads.

Tuft and Chestnut-head were crouching down. They were shifting leaves and blades of grass from the footprints that Fa and Lok had made. Tuft looked up and spoke:

'Tuami.'

Chestnut-head followed the prints with outstretched hand. Tuft spoke to the broad man.

'Tuami!'

The broad man turned to them from the pile of stones and sticks which had occupied him. He threw a quick bird-noise, incongruously delicate, and they answered. Fa spoke in Lok's ear.

'It is his name—'

Tuami and the others were bent and nodding over the prints. Where the ground hardened towards the tree the footprints were invisible and when Lok expected the new men to put their noses to the ground they straightened up and stood. Tuami began to laugh. He was pointing towards the fall, laughing and twittering. Then he stopped, struck his palms loudly against each other, said one word and returned to the pile.

As though the one word had changed the clearing, the new men began to relax. Although Chestnut-head and Tuft still watched the forest, they stood, each at a side of the clearing, looking over the thorns and their sticks unbent. Pine-tree did not move any of the bundles for a while; he put one hand to his shoulder, pulled a piece of hide and stepped out of his skin. This hurt Lok like the sight of a thorn under a man's nail; but then he saw that Pine-tree did not mind, was glad in fact, was cool and comfortable in his own white skin. He was naked now like Lok, except that he had a piece of deerskin wound tightly round his thin waist and loins.

Now Lok could see two other things. The new people did not move like anything he had ever seen before. They were balanced on top of their legs, their waists were so wasp-thin that when they moved their bodies swayed backwards and forwards. They did not look at the earth but straight ahead. And they were not merely hungry. Lok knew famine when he saw it. The new people were dying. The flesh was sunken to their bones as Mal's flesh had sunken. Their movements, though they had in their bodies the bending grace of a young bough, were dream-slow. They walked upright and they should be dead. It was as though something that Lok could not see were supporting them, holding up their heads, thrusting them slowly and irresistibly forward. Lok knew that if he were as thin as they, he would be dead already.

Tuft had thrown his skin on the ground below the dead tree and was heaving at a great bundle. Chestnut-head came quickly to help him and they lifted together. Lok saw their faces crease as they laughed at each other and a sudden gush of affection for them pushed the heavy feeling down in his body. He could see how they shared the weight, felt in his own limbs the drag and desperate effort. Tuami came back. He took off his skin, stretched, scratched himself and knelt on the ground. He swept a patch bare of leaves until the brown earth showed. He had a little stick in his right hand and he talked to the other men. There was much nodding. The logs bumped and there was a noise of voices by the water. The men in the clearing stopped talking. Tuft and Chestnut-head began to move round the thorns again.

Then a new man appeared. He was tall and not as thin as the others. The hair under his mouth and above the head was grey and white like Mal's. It frizzed in a cloud and under it a huge cat-tooth hung from either ear. They could not see his face for his back was to them. In their heads they called him the old man. He stood looking down at Tuami and his harsh voice dived and struggled.

Tuami made more marks. They joined; and suddenly Lok and Fa shared a picture of the old woman drawing a line round the body of Mal. Fa's eyes flickered sideways at Lok and she made a tiny down-stabbing motion with one finger. Those men who were not on watch gathered round Tuami and talked to each other and to the old man. They did not gesticulate much nor dance out their meanings as Lok and Fa might have done but their thin lips puttered and flapped. The old man made a movement with his arm and bent down to Tuami. He said something to him.

Tuami shook his head. The men went a little way from him and sat down in a row with only Tuft still on watch. Fa and Lok watched what Tuami was doing over the row of hairy heads. Tuami scrambled round the other side of the patch and they could see his face. There were upright lines between his eyebrows and the point of his tongue was moving after the line as he drew it. The line of heads began to twitter again. A man picked some small sticks and broke them. He shut them in his hand and each of the others took one from him.

Tuami got up, went to a bundle and pulled out a bag of leather. There were stones and wood, and shapes in it and he arranged them by the mark on the ground. Then he squatted down in front of the men, between them and the marked patch. Immediately the men began to make a noise with their mouths. They struck their hands together and the noise went with the sharp smacks. The noise swept and plunged and twisted yet always remained the same shape, like the hummocks at the foot of the fall that were rushing water yet always the same in the same place. Lok's head began to fill with the fall as though he had looked at it too long and it was sending him to sleep. The tightness of his skin had relaxed a little since he saw the new people liking each other. Now the flock was coming back into his head as the voices and the smack! smack! went on.

The shattering call of a rutting stag blared just under the tree. The flock left Lok's head. The men had bent till their various heads of hair swept the ground. The stag of all stags was dancing out into the clearing. He came round the line of heads, danced to the other side of the marks, turned and stood still. He blared his call again. Then there was silence in the clearing, while the woodpigeons talked to each other.

Tuami became very busy. He began to throw things on to the marks. He reached forward and made important movements. There was colour on the bare patch, colour of autumn leaves, red berries, the white of frost and the dull blackness that fire will leave on rock. The men's hair still lay on the ground and they said nothing.

Tuami sat back.

The skin that had tightened over Lok's body went wintry chill. There was another stag in the clearing. It lay where the marks had been, flat on the ground; it was racing along and yet, like the men's voices and the water below the fall, it stayed in the same place. Its colours were those of the breeding season, but it was very fat, its small dark eye spied Lok's eye through the ivy. He felt caught and cowered down in the soft wood where the food ran and tickled. He did not want to look.

Fa had his wrist and was drawing him up again. Fearfully he put his eye to the leaves and looked back at the flat stag; but it was hidden for men were standing in front of it. Pine-tree was holding a piece of wood in his left hand and it was polished and there was a branch or a piece of a branch sticking out of the farther side of it. One of Pine-tree's fingers was stretched along this branch. Tuami stood opposite him. He took hold of the other end of the wood. Pine-tree was talking to the standing stag and the flat stag. They could hear that he was pleading. Tuami raised his right hand in the air. The stag blared. Tuami struck hard and there was now a glistening stone biting into the wood. Pine-tree stood still for a moment or two. Then he removed his hand carefully from the polished wood and a finger remained stretched out on the branch. He turned away and came to sit with the others. His face was more like bone than it had been before, and he moved very slowly and with a stagger. The other men held up their hands and helped him down among them. He said nothing. Chestnut-head took out some hide and bound up his hand and both the stags waited until he had finished.

Tuami turned the wooden thing over and the finger lingered, then dropped off with a little plop. It lay on the foxy red of the stag. Tuami sat down again. Two of the men had their arms round Pine-tree who was leaning sideways. There was a great stillness so that the fall sounded nearer.

Chestnut-head and Bush stood up and went near the lying stag. They held their curved sticks in one hand and the red-feathered twigs in the other. The standing stag moved his man's hand as though he were sprinkling them with something, then he reached out and touched them each on the cheek with a frond of fern. They began to bend over the stag on the ground, stretching their arms down and their right elbows were rising behind them. Then there was a flick! flick! and two twigs were sticking in the stag by its heart. They bent down, pulled the twigs out and the stag made no movement. The seated men beat their hands together and made the water-hump sounds over and over till Lok yawned and licked his lips. Chestnut-head and Bush were still standing with their sticks. The stag blared, the men bent till their hair was on the ground. The stag began to dance again. His dance prolonged the sound of voices. He came near; he passed under the tree and out of sight and the voices ceased. Behind them, between the dead tree and the river, the stag blared once more.

Tuami and Tuft ran quickly to the thorns across the trail and pulled one aside. They stood each side of the opening, pulling back, and Lok could see that now their eyes were shut. Chestnut-head and Bush stole forward softly, their bent sticks raised. They passed through the opening, disappeared noiselessly into the forest and Tuami and Tuft let the thorns fall back.

The sun had moved so that the stag that Tuami had made was smelling at the shadow of the dead tree. Pine-tree was sitting on the ground under the tree and shivering a little. The men began to move slowly in the dream sloth of hunger. The old man came out from under the dead tree and began to talk to Tuami. Now his hair was tied tightly to his head and spots of sun slid over it. He walked forward and looked down at the stag. He reached out a foot and began to rub it round in the stag's body. The stag did nothing but allowed itself to be hidden. In a moment or two there was nothing on the ground but patches of colour and a head with a tiny eye. Tuami turned away, talking to himself, went to a bundle and rummaged. He brought out a spike of bone, heavy and wrinkled at one end like the surface of a tooth and fined down at the other to a blunt point. He knelt and began to rub this blunt point with a little stone and Lok could hear it scrape. The old man came close to him, pointed to the bone, laughed in a roaring voice and pretended to thrust something into his chest. Tuami bent his head and went on rubbing. The old man pointed to the river and then to the ground and began to make a long speech. Tuami thrust the bone and stone into the hide by his waist, got up and passed under the dead tree out of sight.

The old man stopped talking. He sat carefully on a bundle near the centre of the clearing. The stag's head with its tiny eye was at his feet.

Fa spoke in Lok's ear:

'He went away before. He fears the other stag.'

Lok had an immediate and vivid picture of the standing stag that had danced and blared. He shook his head in agreement.

The Large Ant

HOWARD FAST

The Large Ant *first appeared in the science fiction magazine* Fantastic Universe *in 1960. It was reprinted by Kingsley Amis and Robert Conquest in* Spectrum IV *in 1965, the introduction to which included a conversation between Amis, C. S. Lewis and Brian Aldiss, themselves writers of science fiction. During their discussion Amis made the following point:*

> *'I think thirty years ago if you wanted to discuss a general point you would go to the historical novel; now you would go to what I might describe in a prejudiced way as science fiction. In science fiction you can isolate the factors you want to examine.'*

This has certainly been true of most of the stories included in this anthology; writers have centred their work on one or more features of human behaviour and as a result allegory or satire can emerge strongly from their narratives; comment, explicit or implicit, is a fundamental quality of good science fiction writing. Jules Verne, Stevenson and H. G. Wells all made their comments in one way or another on the society and time in which they lived. Swift and, in our own time, Golding have used fiction for this purpose even more strongly.

The Large Ant *is in the mainstream of this kind of writing; it is an emphatic statement, possibly too emphatic at times, of Man's unintelligent aggression when he feels threatened. The story begins in a normal, low-keyed setting – fishing, golf and supper – and then explodes into violence; the normal life of Morgan is resumed and the strange nature of the giant ant is explained calmly by scientists in terms which are unemotional and deliberate. By this objectivity Man's violence and not the world of the ant is presented as the unusual, the abnormal – and undesirable – feature of life. The story ends with a recognition of Man's apparent helplessness in the face of his own nature: 'We can't change. We are what we are', and 'Like a criminal who can no longer live with himself, I am content to be judged.' Nevertheless one feels that in the act of confession itself lies the final hope of regeneration.*

There have been all kinds of notions and guesses as to how it would end. One held that sooner or later there would be too many people; another that we would do each other in, and the atom bomb made that a very good likelihood. All sorts of notions, except the simple fact that we were what we were. We could find a way to feed any number of people and perhaps even a way to avoid wiping each other out with the bomb; those things we are very good at, but we have never been any good at changing ourselves or the way we behave.

I know. I am not a bad man or a cruel man; quite to the contrary, I am an ordinary, humane person, and I love my wife and my children and I get along with my neighbours. I am like a great many other men, and I do the things they would do and just as thoughtlessly. There it is in a nutshell.

I am also a writer, and I told Lieberman, the curator, and Fitzgerald, the government man, that I would like to write down the story. They shrugged their shoulders. 'Go ahead,' they said, 'because it won't make one bit of difference.'

'You don't think it would alarm people?'

'How can it alarm anyone when nobody will believe it?'

'If I could have a photograph or two.'

'Oh, no,' they said then. 'No photographs.'

'What kind of sense does that make?' I asked them. 'You are willing to let me write the story – why not the photographs so that people could believe me?'

'They still won't believe you. They will just say you faked the photographs, but no one will believe you. It will make for more confusion, and if we have a chance of getting out of this, confusion won't help.'

'What will help?'

They weren't ready to say that, because they didn't know. So here is what happened to me, in a very straightforward and ordinary manner.

Every summer, sometime in August four good friends of mine and I go for a week's fishing on the St Regis chain of lakes in the Adirondacks. We rent the same shack each summer; we drift around in canoes, and sometimes we catch a few bass. The fishing isn't very good, but we play cards well together, and we cook out and generally relax. This summer past, I had some things to do that couldn't be put off. I arrived three days late, and the weather was so warm and even and beguiling that I decided to stay on by myself for a day or two after the others left. There was a small flat lawn in front of the shack, and I made up my mind to spend at least three or four hours at short putts. That was how I happened to have the putting iron next to my bed.

The first day I was alone, I opened a can of beans and a can of beer for my supper. Then I lay down in my bed with *Life on the Mississippi*, a pack of cigarettes, and an eight-ounce chocolate bar. There was nothing I had to do, no telephone, no demands and no newspapers. At that moment, I was about as contented as any man can be in these nervous times.

It was still light outside, and enough light came in through the window above my head for me to read by. I was just reaching for a fresh cigarette, when I looked up and saw it on the foot of my bed. The edge of my hand was touching the golf club, and with a single motion I swept the club over and down, struck it a savage and accurate blow, and killed it. That was what I referred to before. Whatever kind of man I am, I react as a man does. I think that any man, black, white or yellow, in China, Africa or Russia, would have done the same thing.

First I found that I was sweating all over, and then I knew I was going to be sick. I went outside to vomit, recalling that this hadn't happened to me since 1943, on my way to Europe on a tub of a Liberty Ship. Then I felt better and was able to go back into the shack and look at it. It was quite dead, but I had already made up my mind that I was not going to sleep alone in this shack.

I couldn't bear to touch it with my bare hands. With a piece of brown paper, I picked it up and dropped it into my fishing creel. That, I put into the trunk case of my car, along with what luggage I carried. Then I closed the door of the shack, got into my car and drove back to New York. I stopped once along the road, just before I reached the Thruway, to nap in the car for a little over an hour. It was almost dawn when I reached the city, and I had shaved, had a hot bath and changed my clothes before my wife awoke.

During breakfast, I explained that I was never much of a hand at the solitary business, and since she knew that, and since driving alone all night was by no means an extraordinary procedure for me, she didn't press me with any questions. I had two eggs, coffee, and a cigarette. Then I went into my study, lit another cigarette, and contemplated my fishing creel, which sat upon my desk.

My wife looked in, saw the creel, remarked that it had too ripe a smell, and asked me to remove it to the basement.

'I'm going to dress,' she said. The kids were still at camp. 'I have a date with Ann for lunch – I had no idea you were coming back. Shall I break it?'

'No, please don't. I can find things to do that have to be done.'

Then I sat and smoked some more, and finally I called the museum, and asked who the curator of insects was. They told me his name was Bertram Lieberman, and I asked to talk to him. He had a pleasant voice. I told him that my name was Morgan, and that I was a writer, and he politely indicated that he had seen my name and read something that I had written. That is normal procedure when a writer introduces himself to a thoughtful person.

I asked Lieberman if I could see him, and he said that he had a busy morning ahead of him. Could it be tomorrow?

'I am afraid it has to be now,' I said firmly.

'Oh? Some information you require.'

'No. I have a specimen for you.'

'Oh?' The 'oh' was a cultivated, neutral interval. It asked and answered and said nothing. You have to develop that particular 'oh'.

'Yes, I think you will be interested.'

'An insect?' he asked mildly.

'I think so.'

'Oh? Large?'

'Quite large,' I told him.

'Eleven o'clock? Can you be here then? On the main floor to the right, as you enter.'

'I'll be there,' I said.

'One thing – dead?'

'Yes, it's dead.'

'Oh?' again. 'I'll be happy to see you at eleven o'clock, Mr Morgan.'

My wife was dressed now. She opened the door to my study and said firmly, 'Do get rid of that fishing creel. It smells.'

'Yes, darling. I'll get rid of it.'

'I should think you'd want to take a nap after driving all night.'

'Funny, but I'm not sleepy,' I said. 'I think I'll drop around to the museum.'

My wife said that was what she liked about me, that I never tired of places like museums, police courts and third-rate night clubs.

Anyway, aside from a racetrack, a museum is the most interesting and unexpected place in the world. It was unexpected to have two other men waiting for me, along with Mr Lieberman, in his office. Lieberman was a skinny, sharp-faced man of about sixty. The government man, Fitzgerald, was small, dark-eyed, and wore gold-rimmed glasses. He was very alert, but he never told me what part of the government he represented. He just said 'we', and it meant the government. Hopper, the third man, was comfortable-looking, pudgy, and genial. He was a United States senator with an interest in entomology, although before this morning I would have taken better than even money that such a thing not only wasn't, but could not be.

The room was large and square and plainly furnished, with shelves and cupboards on all walls.

We shook hands, and then Lieberman asked me, nodding at the creel, 'Is that it?'

'That's it.'

'May I?'

'Go ahead,' I told him. 'It's nothing that I want to stuff for the parlour. I'm making you a gift of it.'

'Thank you, Mr Morgan,' he said, and then he opened the creel and looked inside. Then he straightened up, and the other two men looked at him inquiringly.

He nodded. 'Yes.'

The senator closed his eyes for a long moment. Fitzgerald took off his glasses and wiped them industriously. Lieberman spread a piece of plastic on his desk, and then lifted the thing out of my creel and laid it on the plastic. The two men didn't move. They just sat where they were and looked at it.

'What do you think it is, Mr Morgan?' Lieberman asked me.

'I thought that was your department.'

'Yes, of course. I only wanted your impression.'

'An ant. That's my impression. It's the first time I saw an ant fourteen, fifteen inches long. I hope it's the last.'

'An understandable wish,' Lieberman nodded.

Fitzgerald said to me, 'May I ask how you killed it, Mr Morgan?'

'With an iron. A golf club, I mean. I was doing a little fishing with some friends up at St Regis in the Adirondacks, and I brought the iron for my short shots. They're the worst part of my game, and when my friends left, I intended to stay on at our shack and do four or five hours of short putts. You see—'

'There's no need to explain,' Hopper smiled, a trace of sadness on his face. 'Some of our very best golfers have the same trouble.'

'I was lying in bed, reading, and I saw it at the foot of my bed. I had the club—'

'I understand,' Fitzgerald nodded.

'You avoid looking at it,' Hopper said.

'It turns my stomach.'

'Yes – yes, I suppose so.'

Lieberman said, 'Would you mind telling us why you killed it, Mr Morgan.'

'Why?'

'Yes – why?'

'I don't understand you,' I said. 'I don't know what you're driving at.'

'Sit down, please, Mr Morgan,' Hopper nodded. 'Try to relax. I'm sure this has been very trying.'

'I still haven't slept. I want a chance to dream before I say how trying.'

'We are not trying to upset you, Mr Morgan,' Lieberman said. 'We do feel, however, that certain aspects of this are very important. That is why I am asking you why you killed it. You must have had a reason. Did it seem about to attack you?'

'No.'

'Or make any sudden motion towards you?'

'No. It was just there.'

'Then why?'

'This is to no purpose,' Fitzgerald put in. 'We know why he killed it.'

'Do you?'

'The answer is very simple, Mr Morgan. You killed it because you are a human being.'

'Oh?'

'Yes. Do you understand?'

'No, I don't.'

'Then why did you kill it?' Hopper put in.

'I was scared to death. I still am, to tell the truth.'

Lieberman said, 'You are an intelligent man, Mr Morgan. Let me show you something.' He then opened the doors of one of the wall cupboards, and there stood eight jars of formaldehyde and in each jar a specimen like mine – and in each case mutilated by the violence of its death. I said nothing. I just stared.

Lieberman closed the cupboard doors. 'All in five days,' he shrugged.

'A new race of ants,' I whispered stupidly.

'No. They're not ants. Come here!' He motioned me to the desk and the other two joined me. Lieberman took a set of dissecting instruments out of his drawer, used one to turn the thing over and then pointed to the underpart of what would be the thorax in an insect.

'That looks like part of him, doesn't it, Mr Morgan?'

'Yes, it does.'

Using two of the tools, he found a fissure and pried the bottom apart. It came open like the belly of a bomber; it was a pocket, a pouch, a receptacle that the thing wore, and in it were four beautiful little tools or instruments or weapons, each about an inch and a half long. They were beautiful the way any object of functional purpose and loving creation is beautiful – the way the creature itself would have been beautiful, had it not been an insect and myself a man. Using tweezers, Lieberman took each instrument off the brackets that held it, offering each to me. And I took each one, felt it, examined it, and then put it down.

I had to look at the ant now, and I realized that I had not truly looked at it before. We don't look carefully at a thing that is horrible or repugnant to us. You can't look at anything through a screen of hatred. But now the hatred and the fear were dilute, and as I looked, I realized it was not an ant although like an ant. It was nothing I had ever seen or dreamed of.

All three men were watching me, and suddenly I was on the defensive. 'I didn't know! What do you expect when you see an insect that size?'

Lieberman nodded.

'What in the name of God is it?'

From his desk Lieberman produced a bottle and four small glasses. He poured and we drank it neat. I would not have expected him to keep good Scotch in his desk.

'We don't know,' Hopper said. 'We don't know what it is.'

Lieberman pointed to the broken skull from which a white substance oozed. 'Brain material – a great deal of it.'

'It could be a very intelligent creature,' Hopper nodded.

Lieberman said. 'It is an insect in developmental structure. We know very little about intelligence in our insects. It's not the same as what we call intelligence. It's a collective phenomenon – as if you were to think of the component parts of our bodies. Each part is alive, but the intelligence is a result of the whole. If that same pattern were to extend to creatures like this one—'

I broke the silence. They were content to stand there and stare at it.

'Suppose it were?'

'What?'

'The kind of collective intelligence you were talking about.'

'Oh? Well, I couldn't say. It would be something beyond our wildest dreams. To us – well, what we are to an ordinary ant.'

'I don't believe that,' I said shortly, and Fitzgerald, the government man, told me quietly, 'Neither do we. We guess.'

'If it's that intelligent, why didn't it use one of those weapons on me?'

'Would that be a mark of intelligence?' Hopper asked mildly.

'Perhaps none of these are weapons,' Lieberman said.

'Don't you know? Didn't the others carry instruments?'

'They did,' Fitzgerald said shortly.

'Why? What were they?'

'We don't know,' Lieberman said.

'But you can find out. We have scientists, engineers – good God, this is an age of fantastic instruments. Have them taken apart!'

'We have.'

'Then what have you found out?'

'Nothing.'

'Do you mean to tell me,' I said, 'that you can find out nothing about these instruments – what they are, how they work, what their purpose is?'

'Exactly,' Hopper nodded. 'Nothing, Mr Morgan. They are meaningless to the finest engineers and technicians in the United States. You know the old story – suppose you gave a radio to Aristotle? What would he do with it? Where would he find power? And what would he receive with no one to send? It is not that these instruments are complex. They are actually very simple. We simply have no idea of what they can or should do.'

'But there must be a weapon of some kind.'

'Why?' Lieberman demanded. 'Look at yourself, Mr Morgan – a

cultured and intelligent man, yet you cannot conceive of a mentality that does not include weapons as a prime necessity. Yet a weapon is an unusual thing, Mr Morgan. An instrument of murder. We don't think that way, because the weapon has become the symbol of the world we inhabit. Is that civilized, Mr. Morgan? Or are the weapon and civilization in the ultimate sense incompatible? Can you imagine a mentality to which the concept of murder is impossible – or let me say absent? We see everything through our own subjectivity. Why should some other – this creature for example – see the process of mentation out of his subjectivity? So he approaches a creature of our world – and he is slain. Why? What explanation? Tell me, Mr Morgan, what conceivable explanation could we offer a wholly rational creature for this—' pointing to the thing on his desk. 'I am asking you the question most seriously. What explanation?'

'An accident?' I muttered.

'And the eight jars in my cupboard? Eight accidents?'

'I think, Dr Lieberman,' Fitzgerald said, 'that you can go a little too far in that direction.'

'Yes, you would think so. It's a part of your own background. Mine is as a scientist. As a scientist, I try to be rational when I can. The creation of a structure of good and evil, or what we call morality and ethics, is a function of intelligence – and unquestionably the ultimate evil may be the destruction of conscious intelligence. That is why, so long ago, we at least recognized the injunction, "Thou shalt not kill!" even if we never gave more than lip service to it. But to a collective intelligence, such as this might be a part of, the concept of murder would be monstrous beyond the power of thought.'

I sat down and lit a cigarette. My hands were trembling. Hopper apologized. 'We have been rather rough with you, Mr Morgan. But over the past days, eight other people have done just what you did. We are caught in the trap of being what we are.'

'But tell me – where do these things come from?'

'It almost doesn't matter where they come from,' Hopper said hopelessly. 'Perhaps from another planet – perhaps from inside this one – or the moon or Mars. That doesn't matter. Fitzgerald thinks they come from a smaller planet, because their movements are apparently slow on earth. But Dr Lieberman thinks that they move slowly because they have not discovered the need to move quickly. Meanwhile, they have the problem of murder and what to do with it. Heaven knows how many of them have died in other places – Africa, Asia, Europe.'

'Then why don't you publicize this? Put a stop to it before it's too late!'

'We've thought of that,' Fitzgerald nodded. 'What then – panic, hysteria, charges that this is the result of the atom bomb? We can't change. We are what we are.'

'They may go away,' I said.

'Yes, they may,' Lieberman nodded. 'But if they are without the curse of murder, they may also be without the curse of fear. They may be social in the highest sense. What does society do with a murderer?'

'There are societies that put him to death – and there are other societies that recognize his sickness and lock him away, where he can kill no more,' Hopper said. 'Of course, when a whole world is on trial, that's another matter. We have atom bombs now and other things, and we are reaching out to the stars—'

'I'm inclined to think that they'll run,' Fitzgerald put in. 'They may just have that curse of fear, Doctor.'

'They may,' Lieberman admitted. 'I hope so.'

But the more I think of it the more it seems to me that fear and hatred are the two sides of the same coin. I keep trying to think back, to recreate the moment when I saw it standing at the foot of my bed in the fishing shack. I keep trying to drag out of my memory a clear picture of what it looked like, whether behind that chitinous face and the two gently waving antennae there was any evidence of fear and anger. But the clearer the memory becomes, the more I seem to recall a certain wonderful dignity and repose. Not fear and not anger.

And more and more, as I go about my work, I get the feeling of what Hopper called 'a world on trial'. I have no sense of anger myself. Like a criminal who can no longer live with himself, I am content to be judged.